THE WAY

TO

STOREY

L. B. Anne

JOA Press
Florida

Copyright © 2021 L. B. ANNE
All Rights Reserved.

Cover creation by Candi Marshall
Edited by Michaela Bush
Proofread by Jessica Renwick

No part of this publication may be reproduced, stored in a retrieval system, or transmitted, in any form or by any means, electronic, mechanical, photocopying, recording, or otherwise without the written permission of the author.

This is a work of fiction. Names, characters, business, places, events, and incidents in this book are purely fictional and any resemblance to actual person, living or dead, is coincidental.

ISBN: 9781736268810

Southern Florida
Present Day

They say the swamp spit her out.
They were wrong.
Storey did.

THE WAY TO STOREY

Chapter 1

"Lou, grab the tackle box!"

"Coming, Gramps!"

I ran through the house looking for my gray sneakers and found them behind the front door. The bottom of the left one was so worn, I poked at it and my finger went through.

"Lou!"

"Putting my shoes on!" I yelled as I hurried and tied the laces. Barefoot was the way for me, but I'd gotten splinters from our rickety dock, and Gramps's eyes weren't as keen as they used to be. No spending the evening limping around for me—walking on one toe until Gramps found a magnifying glass.

"Lou!"

"I'm right here!" I ran up behind him and placed the rusted box at his feet. It looked as old as Gramps. Maybe as old as his father. But it held his most prized fishing lures, and I used to love to play with them. They were so colorful: blues, greens, reds, and oranges. I guess that's why the fish liked them so much. I got the hook of one of those stuck in my foot once too. After that, Gramps always slapped my hand if I reached for one.

There were hooks, lead weights, fishing line, and a knife in the box too. On the bottom were a few bandages and a tiny bottle of bug repellant.

Gramps glanced at me. "No comb today, Lou?"

I reached up to scratch my scalp, but even with my skinny fingers, I couldn't quite get them through my hair and gave up. "I couldn't find it."

"And your clothes?"

"What's wrong with my clothes?"

"Why is that child dressed like that?" Ma Poo yelled from across the field.

I held out my sleep shirt on the sides and spun around.

"Lord, if you don't get inside and put on some clothes, Luella. . ."

Gramps motioned with his head toward the house. "Get to it."

I took off like a rocket, ran up onto our porch, through the front door, and out the back, grabbing shorts and a t-shirt off the line. If I didn't hurry, Gramps might set out on his jon boat without me.

There was no time to run up to my room. I dressed in the kitchen and kicked my sleep shirt out the back door.

Gramps usually made sandwiches to take out with us. But there weren't any crumbs on the counters. The breadbox wasn't open with the loaf sitting out either.

I looked to the right without turning my head. He didn't think I saw him. Before the back screen door closed, he came in.

Here he comes, he's getting closer. Get ready. My right arm shot out to the side, and I caught him. I never doubted that I could.

He rested in my palm as I walked outside. They never put up a fight. "You know you can't come inside. Don't do it again. Gramps won't be as nice as I am. He'll come for you with a shoe."

Then I whispered to it, "Go over to Ma Poo's. When she turns the porch light on at night, you'll see the way. When she opens the door, fly in. Got it?"

Hearing Ma Poo screaming clear across the field was going to be hilarious.

"I don't do bugs," she'd always said when she called us over just to remove a daddy longlegs.

"But stay away from here," I said and set the palmetto bug on the ground. "Go! Roaches don't belong inside."

If Gramps had known I'd done that, he would've washed me clean with bleach. So no matter how proud I was of how fast I moved, I decided not to share that I was the fastest bug catcher that ever lived.

I rubbed my hand over my shorts, went back inside, grabbed two apples, and ran out the front door.

Guess who was still out there? "Much better," Ma Poo yelled. "Come over here so I can do something to that head."

"Maybe later," I yelled back.

"I've got something for you, too!"

"Tadpoles?" I asked, ready to charge over to retrieve my gift.

"Why on earth would I have tadpoles? Guess again!"

I couldn't. I only wanted tadpoles.

"Glitter!"

"Thank you, Ma Poo!" She wasn't supposed to mention that in front of Gramps. It was the last thing I needed for the birthday gift I was making for him.

Gramps hopped down from the dock to the bank alongside it. After he loaded our boat, I hopped in. He grimaced as he pushed it out. I'm only eleven, I don't think I weighed too much, but Gramps was really strong.

I was excited about the day's catch. We usually came home with about five fish. "Good eaten," Gramps would say as he held up a huge bass.

But the best part of going fishing was listening to Gramps's stories while we sat in the middle of the lake, watching the waves as we waited on that first tug of the line.

I've lived with Gramps my whole life. I don't remember much about my parents or the accident that took them from me. Gramps said when the police found me, I was strapped in the back in my car seat, looking up at them just as bright as you please, without a care in the world.

But what I do remember is a voice. It told me everything was going to be okay.

I've mentioned it to Gramps before. "Great day," he said as he stared at me. His way of saying *you don't say* or *oh my goodness, wow*, or *I can't believe it*. "That's what makes our kind special."

"Our kind?"

And just like that, he was off to his truck. He only answered the questions he wanted to answer, when he wanted to answer them. I was used to it.

But Gramps worried a lot. I noticed it more as I got older.

"You're going to live forever, Gramps," I told him. He glanced up at me and then back at the little white box of worms and picked one up. It wiggled and curled. I bet it knew it was about to be pierced with a hook and thrown into a liquid abyss until a creature snuck up on it and ate it. I always imagined those types of things.

"The three of us. You, me, and Ma Poo. Forever."

"You, Ma Poo, and I; I think is right," he replied, but he didn't deny it.

Ma Poo was our only neighbor. She lived in the double-wide trailer alongside our land. She fussed over me and always worried about Gramps. We shared meals and Gramps's truck. It was old and rusty, and we argued about the color. Gramps said it was gray, while Ma Poo and I insisted it was blue. "Men are color blind," she'd whispered while Gramps' back was turned.

Gramps cast out his line and set down his rod, looked out over the lake, and breathed in deeply. "This is good. This is good," he said while slightly nodding. The lake was his favorite place too. He pulled his straw hat down over his forehead. He once had a head full of curls. A curly afro. I'd seen it in photos. Now, he brushed it with a part on the side and it laid flat.

I handed him an apple. "Gramps, tell me where we're from again."

"You mean Storey?"

"Yeah, tell me about it."

"I've told you all I know."

"No, you haven't."

"You know the important stuff."

"Test me." I sat up. I'd been leaning back on a cushion, scanning the shore for gators. "I'm ready."

"How do you get to Storey?" he asked.

"Follow the birds."

"That's right, always follow the birds. When something seems wrong or off, they feel it first. Follow them."

"One point for Luella. Zero for Gramps."

"I'm not being tested. You are. Where do you keep your feelings?"

I tapped my striped t-shirt over my chest. "Right here."

"That's right, or things will happen."

"That's two for me. You need to try and trip me up, Gramps."

"Where is our secret place?"

"In the field behind our house. Gramps, that has nothing to do with Storey."

"Okay, you caught me, so you win. I'll tell you a bit more."

"Yes!" I exclaimed in triumph.

"Storey is a magical place, where the people dress in gold and jewels. And they're tall. Taller'n anyone you ever saw."

"Why aren't you tall?"

"It's the gravity. We were born here. It keeps us smaller."

I chuckled. "I don't believe it. That doesn't make any sense. Why aren't there more people from Storey?"

"Because they all went back. Someone had to stay behind and assure the gate closed."

"And that's you."

"That was our family," he said and took a bite of his apple. I took a bite of mine too.

"Gramps! The line."

He grabbed his pole with patience and grace.

"Easy, easy. . ." I told him.

"Shush. I know what I'm doing."

"I bet it's a bluegill."

"More likely a bass. Whoa!"

"What's wrong?"

"It's a big'un," Gramps said.

I scooted closer to him. "You're letting 'em run out too far. Reel 'em in!"

"Hush, Lou. I've got this. It needs to drag a little."

"Gramps, look! The other rod!"

"Grab it!"

I picked it up.

"Now, do just like I've taught you."

"I'll bring 'em in. I promise." We were almost back-to-back, pulling and reeling. "Mine's a big one too, Gramps!"

"Can you handle 'em?"

"I've got it." I tucked my lips in, planted my feet, and slightly bent my knees as Gramps reeled in his bass. "Let me see."

"No, keep your eyes on yours."

"I bet it's a turtle, a snapper."

Gramps reached over the side of the boat. "Well, looka there," he said and pulled up my catch with his gloved hand.

"Great day. . ." My eyes were like saucers. I was downright proud.

"You were right. It is a big one. Bigger'n mine," he said. "This will make for some good eating tonight."

"Let's go back and show Ma Poo."

"Not yet. Let's see if we can get a couple more for our fry."

And we did get more. Four, to be exact.

Gramps rowed us to shore, pulled the boat in, and I hopped out onto the sand. I tried to lug the bucket of fish, but it was too heavy.

"Give me that. You're splashing water everywhere. You get the rods."

"Ma Poo," I called. I held out the Poo part real long and high pitched. That's what always got her attention. But she didn't come out with a "Stop that hollerin!"

"Where is she?"

"I don't know," said Gramps, glancing toward her trailer. "We'll hear from her soon enough, once she gets a whiff of this fish frying."

"Yep, that usually does it, just like when I smell her cobbler."

I waited for her, even sat in the rocking chair after dinner, looking over at her place. I started to go over there, but Gramps stopped me. "Everyone needs space every now and again."

I understood that, but still, Ma Poo never showed up. Space was one thing. Fish night was different.

Chapter 2

In Florida, with the sunrise on a warm spring morning comes the chirping of birds so loud and lively, you'd think they were having a party. And sometimes, there's a fog so thick you can't see through it. That's the only time Gramps didn't want me wandering around. He said I might get lost in the swamp. But I knew my way around the swamp as well as my own face.

Gramps was usually up before me. He took early morning walks for exercise. Once, when I'd watched him from my bedroom window, I'd seen him walking along our property line. He stopped every few steps and never looked up from his feet. I asked him what he'd been doing. "My private time is my private time," was all he said.

The smell of breakfast cooking always brought me downstairs, where I'd find Gramps frying bacon or scrambling eggs Ma Poo brought over from her hens. Ma Poo said the happiest hens laid the most eggs. Hers were real happy.

I bounded down the stairs, smelling peaches. Gramps was making corn cakes.

"Morning, Gramps," I said and sat at the table.

His back was to me. "Wash your face, comb your hair, and come back down, properly."

"Aww. . ." He hadn't seen me, but he knew I hadn't done any of it.

"Don't sass me. The food isn't going anywhere. It's not even ready."

I trudged up the stairs to the bathroom. I should've let Ma Poo comb my hair, but it hurt so bad. "Sit still," she'd say. But I *was* sitting still. How could she even tell when she was yanking me every which way? Then she'd give a huge sigh, and the smell of warm boiled peanuts would insult my nose. She always said they gave her gas, but she'd munch on them anyway. After that, she'd go on about me needing to eat more.

People said I was as thin as a rail. "And all muscle," Gramps would add. I was just as strong as any of 'em.

I rubbed my wet washcloth over my face and scrubbed over the white line of sleep that extended from my eye to my temple. Gramps was right. It looked better clean. Olive skinned, Ma Poo had called me. I'd seen olives. I didn't look like them. For a long time, I thought I was green but didn't know it.

I brushed my hair, but as usual, it wouldn't lay down. Though I looked all over the place, I couldn't find my comb to detangle it. It must have disappeared into the land of lost items. That's what I called the bin under my bed. When I cleaned my bedroom in a hurry, I grabbed my mess of papers, crayons, rocks I'd painted, and whatever else, and threw them into the bin. Then I'd slide it under my bed. Chores done.

I pulled back my hair, put a hair tie around it, and let my ponytail hang loose. Long and thick, that was the hair I had. Like my mom, Gramps said.

I dressed in the one striped t-shirt I wore all the time instead of the other four and jean shorts.

"Tahdah!" I exclaimed when I entered the kitchen.

"Much better. Have a seat," said Gramps.

I placed three corn cakes on my plate and covered them in peach compote. Just as I took my first bite, Ma Poo charged through the front door.

"My word, do I smell peaches?"

"Gramps made corn cakes."

"Sit down," said Gramps, placing a plate in front of an empty seat.

"I got back late last night, and do you know what happened?" she asked as she sat.

"What?"

"A palmetto bug flew in. Right at my face. Look here."

I giggled and moved closer, examining the red spot she pointed at.

"This is no laughing matter, young lady."

I glanced up at Gramps, who was trying to hide his amusement. "I'm sorry. What's that mark?"

It was just below the gray streak in her black hair that the humidity had puffed up almost to a huge afro.

"It's where I slapped myself in the head."

Gramps couldn't hold back any longer. He burst with laughter, and I joined him.

"Laugh it up," said Ma Poo, annoyed with us but on the brink of laughter herself.

"You outdid yourself," she said after dabbing her fork in the peach compote and licking it off. "You know what I'm making today?" she asked.

"What?" I asked. It was going to be good. I could tell. She was excited to tell us.

"Chitterlings!"

I stood with my plate, took it to the sink, and ran water over it. "See you guys later."

"Oh, you don't want to talk about chitterlings and where they come from, Lou?" asked Ma Poo. She chortled at herself.

"No more than you want to discuss what a palmetto bug really is," I replied and skirted away and out the back door before she could swat at me.

I ran all the way down our road, hopped the fence, and ran through the next field.

"Lou! You're always running!"

"It's what I'm good at," I said as I slowed and looked up at the sky. "I can smell the rain. You, Stooby?"

He caught up to me. "Not like you can, I reckon."

I bumped him, pushing him into the weeds, and he ran over and bumped me back. We continued like that for a while.

"You smell different," I joked.

"No, I don't."

"You smell like chickenpox."

"Quit it, Lou. I'm not contagious anymore. I thought I'd never get out of the house again." He picked up a stick and hit it along the road as we walked.

"You and sticks. Remember that time you touched that snake on accident?"

"I was reaching for a stick."

"Yeah, you about pooped your pants."

Stooby turned red. "Unh-uh! I did not!"

I only had one friend, not because we lived too far from everyone else, but because of the way the other kids treated me. They didn't like me. There weren't many of us around here, so you'd think we would all stick together.

I grabbed Stooby's arm. "Follow me."

We got on all fours and crawled to the creek. The grass was soft under my hands and knees and still a little wet with dew. "Do you see them?"

"They're down there all right. We should go. I heard Ronnie put a hurting on Alonzo the other day."

"They can't even see us. Don't be a fraidy-cat, Stooby."

"I'm not. We can do other stuff."

"I just want to get closer and see what they're doing."

"Uh-oh! Lou, look. They're coming."

"Run! Come on, Stooby!"

He trotted along as though his shoes were too big. He never could run as fast as I could. If I told him once, I told him a thousand times. All that food he ate all the time, cakes and candy, it slowed him down. Not to mention he was bursting at the seams. Your hips can't move well when you have to run, and your pants are that tight.

"We're gonna get you, Stripes!"

I slowed and reached for Stooby's hand to try and pull him along.

"Don't worry about me. You're the one they want. Keep going!" he yelled.

"I'll see ya!" I pumped my legs as fast as they would go. Gramps called me a natural-born cheetah. I ran all the way home without stopping—barely even breathing.

I charged into the backyard.

Gramps greeted me. "Whoa there, Nelly."

Once I stopped running, I was out of breath, sucking in air between words. "I'm." Breath. "Not." Breath. "A horse."

"Rest a bit."

"Gramps." Breath. "The kids make fun of me."

"Why?"

"Because I wear stripes all the time. You said I wear stripes because I'm special. They don't act like I'm special. They act like I'm a freak."

"Don't use that word round here. You know better."

"Sorry."

"I thought you liked stripes."

"Yes, because you said my mama always wore them."

"She did. Are you supposed to change because of what someone else thinks?"

"Well, no."

"Can a tiger change its stripes?"

"No."

"A tiger doesn't change his stripes. You're a tiger. Be who you are."

I'm a tiger. I like it. Gramps was right. I was proud of who I was and if anyone had anything to say about it, I wouldn't only wear striped shirts or socks but striped pants too.

...

The next day, I followed those kids again—without Stooby. He'd only slow me down or lecture me like he was an adult. "Mind your business, we're not testing out poison ivy to see if it's really poisonous, you don't need to know what dirt tastes like, put your shoes back on. . ."

This time, the boys weren't at the creek. As I snuck closer, I saw that Ronnie had a BB gun. He was my age and always in trouble.

"What are we going to do with them?" asked Cree.

"Fry'em up."

What do they have? Chickens?

"That chest meat is good," said another boy.

Ronnie pointed at each of them. "You do the pluckin', you gut, and I'll wash. Then we'll hand them over to Ma."

I followed to see what they were up to. A moment later, a shot rang out and I stopped moving. I waited to hear where it was coming from and sprinted off. I got there before the other boys and hid.

"I got one," an older boy exclaimed.

"Where? I don't see it," said Ronnie.

He pointed. "Go that way."

I wanted to see the wild chicken and ran, staying low. This was exciting. Most people went to stores for their meat, but they were actually hunting chickens. Or was it turkeys?

My smile turned to a frown, seeing the dead robin.

"Good shot. Bag 'em, Cree."

I covered my ears and cringed. The birds were crying out. Couldn't they hear it too?

While the boys listened to Cree's bragging, I circled back and found their BBs and put the containers in a hole. *Let's see them try to shoot another bird now*, I thought.

The boys came back, searching all over for their BBs. "Where did they go? They were right here," said Ronnie.

"Look!"

I stood atop a huge oak trunk. "We don't kill birds. We need them."

"Get her!"

I ran, leaping over shrubs and landing with my feet barely touching the ground. By the time they got to where they thought I was, I came up behind them.

"Where did she go?"

"Yoo-hoo!" I waved.

"How did she do that?"

"I don't know. She found a shortcut. Go get her!" said that ornery Ronnie.

"No, you go get her."

They pushed each other. I shook my head. "Well, what are you going to do? Is someone going to get me, or what?"

They charged at me. I waited until they were almost there, close enough to grab me—close enough that I could smell the sweat and sunblock on one of them. Ronnie even had his arm outstretched, his hand ready to close on me, but I dashed off, and he fell face-first onto the dirt path.

I wasn't surprised when Sheriff Caldwell showed up at our house that evening. Our gate was locked, but Gramps said it was the law that he had a key.

"Stay inside," Gramps said as he went out to meet him.

"We heard tell Luella is out there messing with the town kids again."

Ronnie climbed out of the passenger side of the patrol car.

"Did not!" I yelled from inside.

"Quiet!" said Gramps.

"Yeah, we were minding our own business," said Ronnie. He wore a small pink bandage over his nose and a larger one on his forehead. That fall scraped him up good.

"Like the time you trapped her like an animal in that hole you boys dug in the ground?" asked Gramps. "Then one of you covered it with palm leaves? Did you tell your father here how you tricked her and left her there?"

He didn't respond.

"Get in the car," demanded Sheriff Caldwell.

Ronnie sulked as he got back in the front seat.

"This is a misunderstanding. I'll talk to the boy."

"She's one little girl, but he's out there with—how many boys does he hang with? Think about it. Who do you think is in the wrong?"

Sheriff Caldwell responded with a slow nod and got in the patrol car.

Gramps watched them as they pulled away.

Ma Poo stood behind him with her arms crossed. "Why didn't you tell me they'd had her trapped in a hole like an animal. How did you find her?"

"She sent a robin. It led me to her."

"I don't know why you keep her around here. It's too dangerous."

"Don't you worry about Lou. She's smarter and stronger than any of 'em."

Why would it be dangerous?

I joined them outside. They were so engrossed in conversation that if it weren't for the screen door slamming behind me, they wouldn't have known I was there. "Why don't they want me around, Gramps?"

"Because of something you did years ago."

Chapter 3

"She doesn't belong here," Ma Poo told Gramps. I'd heard her, and it hurt my feelings.

I'd asked him about it, and he said the same thing he always says, "You *don't* belong here. That's why we need to get you back to our kind."

As I stood over him, atop his bed in my sleep shirt, holding a dead cottonmouth snake, I know he remembered those words too. *"She doesn't belong here."*

Gramps looked frightened for a moment. "What are you doin'?"

"I caught it. It was in your room."

He sat up. "How did you know?"

"I heard it slide across the floor."

"You heard it?"

"I woke and I-I told you earlier something didn't feel right—like someone was here."

My arms dropped. I thought he'd be proud of me. I saved him from a poisonous snake. But he looked bewildered.

"What's wrong?"

"Nothing. I worry what I would do without you."

That was the day I started counting his fibs—which I wasn't allowed to do. But why would Gramps lie to me?

...

I didn't rush down the stairs to breakfast the next morning. I wasn't in the mood to eat with an ungrateful person. If someone had saved my life, I would've treated them like a hero. He acted like I was green with warts and wings or something.

I sat on the end of my bed, picking at the threads that were sticking up from my quilt, thinking. Then I switched to picking at the scab of an old scar on my leg.

Before I went downstairs, I washed my face, dressed, and brushed my hair without Gramps having to tell me. I sat in my usual chair across from his and waited silently.

Gramps was at the stove. He looked back at me. I stared at the table, glanced up at him, and back at the table.

"It was a good thing you did last night. A very good thing."

Why didn't you say that last night, so I wouldn't be sad? I thought. "I was surprised it was inside the house," I mumbled.

"Anywhere a snake can fit, is where it will be."

"Umm-hmm." I didn't say much else.

Gramps set a bowl of oatmeal in front of me. I expected something extra special after the way I was treated. Biscuits and gravy or something. At least he put honey on it.

"No brown sugar today, Lou. We're out."

"Doesn't matter. I don't even like sugar."

Gramps knew I was lying but he didn't say anything. And I acted like there was nothing more important than how well I could stir the honey into my oatmeal.

That afternoon, I headed to town. Gramps said our town was a place that time forgot and that most of the world wasn't nice, but this town was.

It was about a forty-five-minute walk. I didn't mind. The ground still had spots revealing it rained the night before, so I wore my boots. Plus, our land held rainwater as if it would never let it go.

Not far from our property, I walked through a small community of cinder block houses that were never finished. They were covered in foliage and debris from when someone started dumping stuff there. Past that was a sign letting you know where you were—Whispering Isle. But there was no Isle. I couldn't figure out why it was called that. Maybe that's why nothing got finished. It would've been nice to have other neighbors nearby, though.

I kicked an empty soda can all the way into town.

"Lou, what are you doing out of school?" asked Mr. Briggs.

"I don't go."

Mr. Briggs ran the post office/convenience store. He wore his usual gray shirt and navy pants and when he didn't have customers, he often stood outside. He leaned against the wall and hiked up his pant leg to scratch above his ankle. The rash of red spots looked like flea bites to me.

"Oh. That's right. You're homeschooled." He looked at my mud-caked boots. "What else is your grandfather teaching you? How to catch rattlesnakes? Wrestling gators?" He laughed.

I laughed too. "Maybe," I said as I hopped up on the hood of a car that had been parked outside the shop for as long as I could remember and never moved an inch. The hood was scalding hot from the sun, and I forgot I had on shorts, so I scooted to the shaded part. "I bet I could wrestle a gator if I had the gumption."

Mr. Briggs reached inside the window. "Here's a soda for ya, Lou."

"Thanks."

He used a key to pop off the top.

"Thanks."

I bet he was glad to have a little company. No one was ever around.

I took a huge swallow. The cold soda felt good flowing down my throat on such a warm day.

"I've got to get back inside in case someone calls. Tell your grandpa I said hello, hear?"

"I will, Mr. Briggs."

I knew he was really hurrying inside because loudmouth Ruby was coming. I hopped off the car, gulped down the last of the orange soda, and belched. I laughed. "Just a little gas," I said like

Gramps would've, and then headed toward the main highway.

"Who is that?" the woman with Ruby asked before Mr. Briggs could return to his counter inside.

"They say the swamp spit her out."

"Someone needs to take a comb to that head."

I grinned and skipped away. People always wondered where I came from. I grabbed my ponytail. It wasn't much of a ponytail. It started out as one, but after I'd had my lesson and ran around the swamp, it came apart. Now it was a mass of kinky hair, strands falling every which way, with only the end in a braid.

I looked both ways and ran across the highway. I don't know why I ran like Ronnie and those boys were after me. We saw more semi-trucks passing through than anything, but even those were scarce today.

I ran straight up to the library. Well, really the city hall/library.

"How can I help you today, Luella?" asked the woman who always sat at the front desk.

"I need to do some research."

"Do you know how to use a computer?"

"I know well enough," I lied. I didn't want her sitting with me the whole time, because that's what she would do, and Gramps said we weren't supposed to talk about Storey with anyone, ever.

She turned it on. "Let it warm up a second. I keep asking for a newer model, but I'm told it isn't in the budget. You came in at a good time. Usually, there's a line to use it." She kept talking. I figured she gets bored by herself, waiting for a council meeting or someone to visit.

She placed her fingers over the keys of the keyboard. Four on one side and four on the other. Her thumbs were over the long bar in the center. "What are you looking up?"

"I can do it," I said. She rose from the seat, and I placed my fingers over the keyboard just as she had.

She smiled down at me. "All right, then. I'll leave you to it."

In the center of the screen was the word, *Search*. I removed my fingers from the keyboard and typed with one finger. S. T. O. R. E. Y. Gramps taught me it was spelled differently than a story in a book. The screen went white for a moment, then I read:

A storey or story is any level part of a building with a floor that could be used by people.

There were images of buildings with floors and no walls.

I slumped in my chair. That wasn't what I was looking for at all, but that's what I got. There was nothing else, and computers knew everything. Storey didn't exist. There was no other explanation. Gramps made it up. We weren't different. We weren't special. We were weirdos.

A light flashed on the computer, and the screen on the monitor started going crazy. Lines zipped from left to right across the screen and flashed in and out.

"Mrs. Glenn," I called and pointed at the monitor. "It's broken."

"That would be very hard to do," she said as she rushed over. "I've been watching you the whole time. You hardly touched it." I stood, and she slipped into the seat.

"Do you see that light?"

"What is. . ."

She put her finger over a red dot on the monitor. "Go and knock on Mr. Lewiston's door. Tell him to get over here right now."

I ran down the corridor yelling, "Mr. Lewiston!" and banged on each door I passed.

"What's going on out here?"

"Come quick."

He followed me back to the computers. I ran as he limp-walked. Maybe that was running for him.

"Someone was watching this girl while she was on the computer!" said Mrs. Glenn.

Chapter 4

Mr. Lewiston's belly was almost too big for him to sit in the chair. I had the urge to place my ear on it and knock to see if it sounded hollow.

"Not in my library," he said, turning red.

The light blinked off.

"I think they're gone," said Mrs. Glenn.

"Did you see anything?" he asked me.

"Only the screen going crazy."

Mrs. Glenn looked worried. "Maybe someone is trying to tap into our system."

"Get Caldwell on the line and unplug that thing."

"Can I go?" I didn't want to see the sheriff after him coming out to our house about Ronnie.

"It should be okay. We know where to find you if we need you."

...

The things Mrs. Glenn and Mr. Lewiston were saying about the computer were like words from another planet. I didn't understand any of it.

We didn't own a computer. Gramps got all my schoolwork directly from the school. He said we didn't get internet service where we lived and barely got phone service. We kind of liked it that way. We didn't have a television, but Ma Poo did, and a satellite. I watched movies with her sometimes. Evenings, Gramps and I read lots of books—often to each other.

When I got home, I didn't tell Gramps about what happened at the library because he didn't know I'd gone there. Plus, if I told him I tried to look up Storey, he would've been so sore with me.

Sheriff Caldwell didn't come by that evening to question me, so I thought I could forget the whole thing ever occurred. But from that day forward, there were strange happenings. One evening, we were all together out back, sitting at the picnic table having an early supper. Ma Poo buttered a thick slice of homemade bread and handed it to me. Then Gramps and I looked out into the distance. We did it at the same time, as if we'd planned it. Both of us peered out over the swampland beyond the property. Gramps even stood. He looked down at me, and I looked up at him.

"Did you see that?" I asked.

"See what?" asked Ma Poo.

"It's getting closer," said Gramps.

"What's getting closer?"

He didn't respond. The man who never stirred from ease held a hint of worry. He once told me that one day we'd have to leave Osowaw City. I had a feeling that time was getting near.

I asked him later, "Why will we have to leave our home?"

"We're different," said Gramps. "But there are more like us in Storey."

That's all he told me. I wanted to know how we were different and why. Why weren't there more people like us?

Gramps walked away. I wanted to follow behind him, asking a thousand questions like I did when I was little. Why does the floor creak? Why does Stooby have freckles? Could he buy me some? Back then, Gramps could shut me up with a popsicle. That didn't work anymore.

Now, he gave a forbidding gaze and asked, "Do you want to spend the day in your room?"

"No."

"Then hush up."

I hushed, but it wasn't over. The next day, I awoke early and waited until Gramps left for his morning walk. He thought I was still asleep. I heard him open my door some and look in. As soon as I heard the front door close, I hopped off my bed and hurried downstairs.

I searched the house, trying to find anything that would lead me to Storey. There weren't many places to hide things in the front room, so I started there. I opened the bureau drawers, looked under all the furniture, inside chests, and then ran up to Gramps' bedroom, across from mine.

I crawled under his bed and came out covered in dust. But I found a small box. It was wooden with gold designs on the lid. I sat on the floor with my back against his bed frame and opened it. A couple of folded papers, money (in languages I didn't understand), and old coins were the only contents. I picked up each coin and examined it. One had a woman with a baby on her back on it. I liked that one and started to put it in my pocket. It made me think of me and the mother I didn't remember. But I put it back in the box and slid it back where I'd found it, behind a bin of sweaters.

I stood and looked around the room. Gramps's closet was small, and he didn't have much more clothes than I did. I checked all the pockets and every nook. Then I checked his small secretary desk, as he called it. It was really old. I opened the little drawers and slid my hand under the bottoms in case something had been taped underneath. I still didn't find anything. The last place to look was Gramps's dresser. That was too easy. No one would hide anything in the first place someone would look. I fell back on his bed.

"Storey!" I shouted in frustration.

From the corner of my eye, I saw a flash and sat up.

One of the dresser drawers was outlined in light. Something inside of it glowed.

I carefully walked over to it. The light pulsed a little. I reached for the drawer handle as if it might be hot to the touch and pulled it open the slightest bit. The light disappeared. I couldn't see anything inside. Rather than continuing to pull it, I put my fingers inside to guide the drawer open.

SLAM!

I screamed out from the pain that shot up my hand and brought my throbbing red fingers to my mouth.

"What are you doing going through my things?"

"I—I was just..." I wailed from the pain.

Gramps acted like he didn't notice my tears and shot me his "answer me" look.

I sniffed and wiped my eyes. "I don't believe Storey exists."

"Since when?"

"Since now. I was looking for evidence. Why isn't it a place I can see?"

"You can't see the stars during the day, but they are still there. That's how Storey is."

"And it's a stupid name. Why won't you tell me the truth?"

Gramps ignored me and walked away. And that made me angry.

I followed him downstairs. "If you won't let me see what's in there, I'm going to leave. I'm going to run away!" I said while stomping my foot.

"Promise?"

I grabbed the ice pack he handed me and ran out the front door. I ran all the way to Ma Poo's house.

"Ma Poo! It's me!" I yelled as I rang the doorbell. It was early, but I knew she was up. Probably out back with the hens.

The front door swung open.

"Mercy me, why all the tears?" She looked past me at my house and then up the road.

"Gramps closed a drawer on my fingers."

"He did what?"

"He didn't want me to see what was inside." At the time, I forgot the part about me sneaking around in his things.

"Come in here," she said, holding the door open. "Let me have a look." She lifted the ice pack from my hand. "It's not too bad. Sit down. The skin isn't even punctured."

She blew warm air over my fingers. I didn't know how that was supposed to help, but I enjoyed the attention.

"What's gotten into Leon?"

"I don't know." I sniffed.

"All of this happened this morning, before breakfast?"

"I didn't have breakfast."

"You? Go have a seat at the table."

I walked into the kitchen of her doublewide trailer. I didn't know why it was called that. Looked just like a house to me. But during hurricanes, she never stayed in it. She collected her most valuable items in a suitcase and box and stayed at our house until the worst of it passed.

Ma Poo made toast and slathered it in butter and strawberry jam. I scarfed down the two slices, and she made me two more. My left hand held the toast while my right hand rested atop the table under the ice pack.

"While you're here," she said, and I wasn't surprised, "I'm going to do something I've been needing to do for a while now."

After I'd eaten, she patted the counter. "Right here, missy."

I lay back on Ma Poo's countertop as she washed my hair. The warm water and the scrubbing of my scalp felt so good, I forgot all about my hand.

"Is this what a spa feels like?" I asked.

"You think I know?

"I used to lay you up here like this when you were little. Even bathed you in this here sink. Now you have to bend your knees to fit on the counter."

She went to humming as she worked her way from my roots to my ends. My hair is as strange as people find *me*. It's long, very thick, and three different ways. Straight, wavy, and curly like it doesn't know what it wants to be.

My neck was atop a towel. Ma Poo reached under me and pulled it out so it could cover my sopping wet hair. I hopped off the counter and allowed her to guide me to her living room sofa.

"Sit," she said.

I lowered to the floor, and she sat on the couch behind me. I suppose when someone goes to the dentist and sees all the instruments laid out that the doctor is going to use, it scares the willies out of them. I wouldn't know. I'd never been to a dentist, but I saw it on television. That's how I felt seeing Ma Poo's brush, comb, hair pick, hair ties, hair clips, and bottles of stuff. I think I was going to need some laughing gas like at the dentist.

"My hand hurts," I whined for sympathy. I thought it would make her take it easy on me.

She turned on the television. "You'll be okay. Watch *I Love Lucy*. She can take your mind off everything."

I didn't hear a thing Lucy said. After one hour, six tissue papers from blowing my nose from crying, a swat from Ma Poo with a comb because I tried to get away, Ma Poo having to give her arms a rest, and a wad of fluffy shedded hair the size of a tennis ball that Ma Poo wouldn't allow me to keep and play with later, I looked in the mirror. "That's me?"

"That's you," she replied.

My hair hung in connected braids. Parted down the center, the front braid on the right was braided into the center braid. The center was braided into a braid at the bottom, which hung past my shoulders. My hair was the same on the left. If I'd worn a hat, you'd think I only had two braids. Ma Poo called it plaited.

"Thank you, Ma Poo."

"You're welcome. Your hair is like a sponge. It's going to draw up—shrink a little. But that should last you a while. Leon should pay me a month's wages for that," she joked. "Let's go."

"Where?"

The next thing I knew, she marched me over to my front porch and banged on the screen door. Gramps stood there, looking down at me.

"Well, what do ya know? It's the runaway."

"Runaway?" Ma Poo repeated, instantly a bit sour with me. "What on earth is going on around here?"

I lowered my head and walked inside.

Gramps shook his head. "Oh nothing. The usual. Someone not wanting to follow the rules and then getting mad. Caught her snooping around in my things."

Ma Poo shot me a look. I knew I should have told her. I might not have had a mother and father, but I sure knew what it was like to have them.

"How about you call a truce. It's going to be too hot for moods. Anger only makes you hotter," said Ma Poo.

"What do ya say, Lou?" Gramps held out his hand and I shook it.

Ma Poo was right about it being a hot day. I stayed in the shade as much as possible. The ground seemed to groan for moisture and crack in anger. I didn't even go out to visit Stooby.

Late in the afternoon, Ma Poo and Gramps stood out in the yard. I sat on the porch, peeling a mandarin orange and looked up, hearing a car coming up the dirt road that ended at Ma Poo's property. Then you had to get out of your car and walk the rest of the way across our land if you didn't have a key to the metal fence that blocked off our private road.

"Lou, go inside."

"Yes, sir." I slowly walked away, looking over my shoulder.

"Wash them greens," he said. "Make sure you wash 'em good. We don't want no worms or bugs on the plate tonight."

"Yes, sir."

I stood in the door watching them.

"What you reckon?" asked Ma Poo.

"Fancy cars. They're not from 'round here. Looks like somebody fishing for something."

I ran cold water into a large pan, pushed the greens in, and ran to the front window. The woman and two men who walked into our front yard wore black suits. She pointed at the house and took a step forward. Our sea grape shrub blocked her from view. When it bears fruit, it reminds you of an elephant. The large flat leaves are the ears, and the long thin stem of sea grapes are the nose. They look like clusters of marbles. When they're ripe, we eat them, even though they're mostly pit, or we make them into jam.

I ran up the stairs to the attic and climbed out the window to my perch on the roof. The adults were yelling now.

"She's not going anywhere with you. I've talked to that school. She's fine right where she is," said Gramps.

"Did you just call her an animal?" asked Ma Poo.

"That is not what I said. We're told she runs wild around this place," said the woman.

"Because she likes to be outside and is not planted in front of a television all day?"

"Sir. . ."

"Get off my land."

"Sir. . ."

"Stay right there, I've got something for you."

I climbed back inside and hurried down the stairs. Gramps rushed past me.

"Gramps, what's going on?"

He ignored me and grabbed his shotgun.

"What do they want?"

I ran to the front window, seeing two more cars speed up the road to the house, and Ma Poo's arms flailing as she fussed. She was irate.

Gramps loaded the shotgun and hurried outside with me running behind him, yelling for him to stop. Then we saw that the other cars were police cars.

Gramps turned back to me. "I told your mother I would keep you safe."

"Yes, when I was born. I know."

"Go to our place."

I looked into his brown eyes, now missing the specks of yellow and green I loved. They told me all I needed to know.

I hurried into the house and out the back door. I thought it was normal that we had a hiding place in case of an emergency. Our place was a good distance away, and I ran like the cheetah Gramps always called me and didn't stop until I got there.

I climbed inside Keme. That's what we named her. It means secret. She was an old oak laying on its side. I waited there, hugging my knees.

A shot rang out, and I shuddered. I started to climb out. Gramps might need me. But that wasn't the rule. I knew the rules, even if I had a hard time following them most of the time. I waited, terrified something had happened to him.

The stones and soil around me began to shake.

"Calm down," I told myself. "Keep your emotions inside like Gramps taught you." I rested my head on my knees and my breathing slowed.

Night fell, and the music of the swamp grew louder with frogs, crickets, and the hoot of an owl. But I wasn't afraid. I always felt like I was a part of nature.

A hand grabbed me.

"Gramps!" I crawled toward him and hugged him.

"We're okay. We're okay. Calm down."

He kept saying it, but I didn't believe him. Another fib to add to the list.

"You kept your emotions inside."

"Yes, I did. It was a close one, though."

"I know. I felt it. Let's go home."

We walked in the dark all the way home. I looked up at Gramps as he walked with his arm around me. We both stepped over the root of an oak tree and kept walking. I realized, unlike everyone else, Gramps and I could see where we were going with no lights. And once again, I believed in Storey.

Chapter 5

Ma Poo waited on the back porch, shining a flashlight every which way, even though she knew it would bring bugs. She swatted all around herself. We stopped and watched. She looked like she was having a fit.

"The mosquitos are going to eat her up something awful if we don't hurry," I told Gramps.

"Let 'em. She has enough blood to feed all the mosquitoes in Florida and half the ticks."

We laughed quietly.

"I hear y'all out there!" yelled Ma Poo. "For the life of me, I can't figure how you can find your way home. Unless it was my lamp leading the way."

"It sure was," I fibbed. We all climbed the steps and went inside.

Ma Poo walked into the kitchen. "My nerves are a mess. Make me some tea, Old Man."

"Make your own tea. You know where it is. I need to get this one up to the tub."

This one. Like he had more of me. Wouldn't that be something to see?

...

I ran my bath and listened to the murmured hum of Gramps and Ma Poo's voices. You can tell something about voices, even if you can't make out what's being said. If you hear one and then the other, it's a conversation. But if you hear one, and the other glides into it as if they're joined, they're devising a plan.

I laid my head back in our clawfoot tub. The warm water soothed my muscles. And I was all muscle from what Gramps said. It only took seconds for me to disappear below the waterline, laying at the bottom of the tub looking up. I didn't think about my hair at the time. It was nice not to hear anything for a moment.

After I'd bathed and was tucked in bed, Gramps sat over me.

"I'm sorry I said I didn't believe in Storey, and that I was so mean to you. And. . ." I was afraid to finish, but I had to. "And I need to tell you—"

Gramps shook his head. "I know you didn't mean it."

"No. But—let me finish."

"Lou, you don't have to."

"Yes, I do."

He waited.

"I used the computer at the library."

"For what?"

"To look up Storey."

"You did what? That's the whole reason why all this time, I've kept—" he stood and looked around the room. "What did you find?"

"Nothing, the computer broke."

"Now we know how they found you."

"They? Who? Those people?"

"There are people who look for those from Storey."

"Why?"

"Because we are different."

He sighed and sat again.

"Are we safe?"

"For now." Another fib. I could see the lines forming on his forehead. He was worried. I wanted him to feel better. Why did I always cause him so much stress?

"Will you tell me something about Storey? Where our kind is from?"

Usually, his eyes brightened, and he'd begin by telling me about his youth—going back and forth from here to Storey. But this night he began with, "What is the way to Storey?"

"I don't know." I didn't want to talk about that. I wanted to hear about the place that didn't really seem to exist—how remarkable it sounded. The bright colors and turquoise waters. Images that made me drift off into a magical sleep.

"You do know," said Gramps, being more patient with me than I expected. "What have I taught you?"

He'd always asked about this when we were on our skiff in the middle of the lake. Only now did I realize it was so no one else could hear. Not even Ma Poo.

"Follow the birds."

He grinned. "Yes. Always follow the birds. They know the way. If anything happens to me, get to Storey."

"I don't know if I'd find it, Gramps," I said with a yawn.

"I believe in you."

"I believe in you too, Gramps," I whispered, my eyes closing.

"Listen to your spirit. Listen to your soul. It will guide you." He laid his hand over my chest as he said it and kissed me on the forehead. "You'll get there all right. I'm certain of it."

I opened one eye and watched Gramps leave my room and replayed everything he'd said in my head. He'd said, "you'll get there", not like you would get there if it happened, but you *will* get there.

Gramps had switched on my fan. I kicked off the sheet that covered me, so I could feel the breeze. I closed my eyes, casting off any further thought that I'd have to find Storey. *Ha! Like a kid would really be sent off by herself.*

I woke feeling like I was floating. Then I looked up at Gramps's fuzzy chin. I was in his arms and too groggy to do anything but lay my head against his chest. I couldn't remember the last time he carried me. It was early, hardly any light came through my window—about the time Gramps normally took his walks.

"What are you doing?" I mumbled.

He didn't speak, and that made me nervous. He carried me to my closet, which had no door. Instead of it having a ceiling, you could see clear up into the attic to the trusts of the roof. But just above the inside of the door frame was a shelf you wouldn't know was there unless you'd explored every nook of the house like I had. I didn't know Gramps knew about it.

"Lou, I need you to wake up now. I'm going to hoist you up on this ledge, and you stay there until I come for you, hear?"

"Gramps, what's happened? Did those people come back?"

"Get ready. One. Two. Three." He hoisted me up. I grabbed hold of the cinder block ledge and pulled myself up as he pushed me.

"Don't make a sound," he said.

I lowered my hand and waved so he knew I understood. He grabbed it a moment and squeezed before letting go. His footsteps left the room.

I was just small enough to lay there undetected. It was dusty and I feared I'd sneeze, giving away my hiding place. After a few minutes, I lifted my head, trying to hear.

There wasn't a sound in the house. It was too quiet. I rolled off the ledge and landed with a thud on the closet floor. I waited in case someone had heard me. When no one charged up the stairs, and Gramps didn't run in telling me to get back up there, I went down. I stood to the side of the window nearest the front door and peeked out.

Two men grabbed my grandfather. They forcibly pulled him along. He struggled to fight, but he just wasn't strong enough. They put him in the backseat of their car. *They must've removed the lock from the gate to get their cars back here.*

I ran to the window on the other side of the door, trying to see Gramps better. At first, the car looked empty. Then Gramps's head rose and leaned forward. He looked up at the window. I jumped back, out of view. When I peeked out again, his eyes were still on the window. He may not have seen me, but he knew I was there, because I hardly ever followed directions. He gave his head a slight raise.

I understood and raced up the stairs to my bedroom, ran to the closet, and leaped. I landed on the attic floor. My eyes bulged. Never had I jumped like that before. Running faster than anyone else, yes. Climbing like nobody's business, yes. But jumping ten feet into the air? Since when?

The cinder block shelf was just below me. I lowered myself onto it and backed into the gap, under the attic flooring, pulling my sleep shirt beneath my knees so they wouldn't scrape against the cement. It was a good thing I was so small, or I would've stuck out. I closed my eyes. My breathing was slow and quiet, as if I was barely alive. I believed in my heart I'd become part of the flooring.

The men ransacked our home looking for me. I heard them in Gramps's bedroom, flipping furniture over or tossing things around. Something crashed to the floor. Then they were in my room, and more of them were above me in the attic.

"She's not here," one of the men said.

A voice responded from a radio. "Check everywhere, she's in there."

"We *have* checked everywhere. The old man wasn't lying."

"Then where is she? Check the neighbor's house. Send a team down to the lake."

"Do you think they knew we were coming?"

"Looks that way."

Feet bounded out of the attic and down the stairs, but I didn't move. And it was a good thing. Someone remained, as still as a statue, waiting. As if they thought I was there somewhere and would come out thinking they were gone—which I was. But you couldn't fool me that easily. I could feel him. Much like I could feel that snake in our house. One of them stood perfectly still in each room.

"Clear," someone finally said on the radio, and they left.

I don't know how much time passed before I opened my eyes again and allowed my breathing and heart rate to increase. There were no longer any footsteps above or below me, and no feelings of their presence in our house.

I slid from beneath the wood planks, jumped down from the cinder block ledge, and waited. If I heard the slightest sound—the creak of a floorboard, the brush of a pant leg, a slight breath—I was going to shoot back up to the attic.

From the closet, I looked around my room. There wasn't much sun shining into my window. *It's afternoon?*

My floor was littered with books, games, papers and pens, and my clothes. I quickly changed into shorts, a t-shirt, and socks. I left everything else right where those mean men had tossed them.

I walked with my back along the wall as I went down the stairs, ready to dash upstairs again if I saw anyone. The lower level looked even worse than the upper. I wanted to cry for what they'd done to Gramps' house. All the things he held dear were broken and destroyed. Or thrown around like they were trash. Did they really have to tear everything apart to find me? A broken piece of porcelain sat at my feet. I almost stepped on it. I stooped and ran my finger over the muzzle. Gramps had painted it. *Why did they break this? Did they think I could shrink down and hide in a horse figurine?*

One of my sneakers was near the door and I found the other against the back wall. My hands shook a little as I sat on the bottom step and put them on. But I didn't move from that spot. I sat there, listening to the cold nothingness of the house. Cold was the feeling left behind without Gramps's presence.

What was I going to do? How would I find Gramps? I decided that once it was dark, I'd venture outside and check on Ma Poo.

The sun began to set, casting a gray shadow throughout the room. And with it went the energy our home held that made it feel alive.

I still hadn't moved from that spot when I heard a creak on the porch. The doorknob slowly turned, and the front door opened. No flashlight shined inside. The person had come up in the dark. That meant they could see! *Gramps!*

"Lou," she whispered. "Luella. . ." Ma Poo walked inside holding a broom, ready to wallop someone with it.

I jumped up and ran to her. She looked relieved, as I looked up at her in tears. "They took Gramps."

Chapter 6

Ma Poo held me tight. But it didn't give me the comfort it normally would've. "We've got to get you out of here. They'll be coming back since they didn't find you."

"Your face," I said, reaching up and touching her jaw.

She jerked her head away. "Ouch, that smarts. How can you see me?"

"They did that to you?"

"I'm okay. I'm a strong old woman."

She looked around the room. "It'll be hard to find anything in this mess but grab what you need. Go out the back door and come to my house—from the back. If anyone is watching, we can't leave here together."

"Then they watched you come over here."

"They'd expect me to look for you. They'll wait to see if you leave with me."

"I can't—"

"You can and you will. Get going, missy." Her voice became the more direct, stern tone I was used to, and I ran upstairs for a jacket, my toothbrush, and a change of clothes.

I glanced for the last time into Gramps's room, picturing him sitting on his bed. He'd take off his watch and set it on his nightstand next to his small alarm clock for the night. Everything always in its place. Now, the room was in shambles.

I wiped a tear from the corner of my eye. Where had they taken him? It was all my fault. If I hadn't gone to the library to find more information about Storey, none of this would have happened. We'd be having dinner right now. Fish and cheesy grits. And apple dumplings for dessert. "Doggone Storey," I whispered.

A beam of light shot over the floor. It shone from beneath an overturned dresser drawer. Then it disappeared. I walked closer.

"Storey," I said again, and it lit up. I flipped the drawer over. There was nothing inside. But on the floor was an old gold pocket watch.

The Way to Storey

"Storey," I said once more. The watch emitted a light so bright I had to shut my eyes. I threw myself on top of it and then stuffed it in my pocket. I didn't want anyone to see the light from the windows. I hurried down the stairs, carefully opened the back door, and held it while it closed so it wouldn't slam shut.

Before going to Ma Poo's, I ran to our dock. I had to say goodbye—not to a person, but to my lake and the fish and everything else I was used to seeing out there that made this place my home. I kept my hand in my pocket the whole time, clutching the pocket watch. Then I ran to Ma Poo's house. The back door was open, and she'd unscrewed the lightbulb so it wouldn't turn on when I approached her door.

"What took you so long? I thought I'd have to go back and drag you away." She held my arms and looked into my face. "Listen, honey, I know you like I'd birthed you myself. So I know how you're going to react when I say this."

"What?"

"You—you can't stay here," she said and turned away. Her hand shook as it covered her mouth.

"I know. We're going together."

She shook her head. "I promised your grandfather that if anything happened to him, I'd encourage you to go. He said you would know where. And I don't have to know where, but I need you to do what you promised him. You did promise him, right?"

My lips quivered. "Yes."

"What's are you carrying? Good, you brought your boots. Put them on," she said as she stuffed items in a backpack.

"Right now? I have to go tonight? Gramps said when I hear the birds, but that's in the morning."

Ma Poo stopped moving and sat at her kitchen table. "Then morning it is."

...

I listened to Ma Poo's deep breathing, but I don't believe she slept a wink. She tried to have me sleep in another room, but I didn't want to be alone. So I made a pallet on the floor beside her bed. It was just a foam exercise mat I would never picture her using and a blanket, but it was comfortable.

Ma Poo looked over her mattress at me near the wall and laid back down. It took forever to drift off, because I was so worried about Gramps and my trek the next morning.

I listened to the whirr of Ma Poo's ceiling fan. And I must have fallen asleep, because the next thing I knew, feet were bounding into the room. When I opened my eyes, I didn't know where I was at first.

"Get her up!" a voice said.

I slid over, pulling my blanket with me beneath the bed, and watched their black shoes and slacks and Ma Poo's bare feet.

"Where is she, Winnie?"

Winnie? That's her real name? I liked Ma Poo much better.

"Where's the girl?"

"I told you—"

He held my boots up in front of her. "Are you telling me you can fit these? Show me. Put them on."

He shoved her onto the floor, and our eyes met for a split second.

"She was here, but she ran off."

"She's lying."

"Wait," she yelled with her arm shielding her face. Her bonnet fell from her head. "Do you think you'd find me asleep in my bed if she were here? I told her to get as far away from this place as her legs would carry her."

The man lifted his hand. The back of it was going to come down on Ma Poo!

My breathing quickened. My heartbeat increased. Gramps said to keep my emotions inside. I promised him I would. But I couldn't. Not now. I couldn't hide and let these horrible men hurt Ma Poo.

The floor shifted and the whole doublewide trailer shook.

The men backed up. "Keep your eyes peeled." He spoke into his radio. "She's out there."

Ma Poo looked terrified but wouldn't look in my direction. The men backed out of the room. I slid from under the bed on the side of the room I'd slept on and stood. They saw me, but before they could radio anyone, they and the front wall of the house were ripped away, as well as the men outside.

My legs were weak, and I fell forward, breathing deeply for a moment. I knew something would happen. It always did when I released my emotions, but this... I tore off part of Ma Poo's house.

"Lou," Ma Poo called.

I didn't respond right away. I was ashamed and afraid—afraid of what she thought of me.

"Lou," she said again. I crawled over and reached for her, ready to pull back. But my hand didn't scare her. She grabbed it and allowed me to help her up. "How did you—"

"I'm sorry I broke your house. I didn't fight my emotions like Gramps taught me. I couldn't let them hurt you. I'm sorry."

"Luella, no, you listen here. Don't go getting all sad. And don't you blame yourself. You did what you had to do to help me. That's what we do for those we love. And though you've never said it, I know you do. For the life of me, I don't know how you did this, but I can tell you one thing ...More will come. Do you hear me? When they don't hear from those men, more will come. Maybe even tonight."

She wobbled around the house grabbing items. The floor was so uneven now. She took my hand as though I was the one who needed assistance and walked to where the door should have been and down the stairs. I pulled back.

"Come on. What are you waiting for? We've gotta get out of here."

She said we. I was excited she didn't mean me alone and hurried along with her. She grabbed the keys to Gramps's truck. She had a set too. And we set off.

...

The sun was high when I awoke. Ma Poo hadn't pulled over once, but now she said she needed to. She turned into the parking lot of a diner. I'd slept in my clothes, but she changed in the diner bathroom and returned with coffee and—"What are these?"

"That's a Boston creme donut. Didn't your grandfather ever—never mind. Of course, he didn't. That would've made him too normal."

I took a bite as I watched the sky. The birds were heading east over us. Ma Poo looked up through the windshield at them.

"Luella. . ." she started, as I licked cream from my finger. "This is where we part ways."

My body stiffened and tears welled up in my eyes. "No. Why?"

"What did your grandfather tell you to do?"

"Follow the birds. But you can come too."

"No, I can't."

"Are you afraid I will blow something off again? I promise I won't."

"Look at me, and don't you cry. I mean it. Stop those tears. You're strong and made for this. Your grandfather, that rascal, somehow knew all of this was going to happen. Right down to me leaving with you. Made me promise I'd send you on your way, he did."

I could hear it in her voice. It trembled. This was just as hard for her as it was for me.

A tear fell from her eye.

"Don't cry, Ma Poo."

More tears ran down her cheek. I didn't want her sad or hurting. She was the only family I had left and without me, she'd be safe. "You're right, Ma Poo. I can do this. I'm strong—mostly muscle as Gramps would say. I'm going to find him too."

She sniffed. "Lou, I only want you to do what he told you to do. Promise me."

"I promise. We'll all be together again one day," I said as I put on my backpack. I tried to smile. That's hard to do when you're holding back tears. But I really did believe it. "Where will you go?"

"I have family up north."

I opened the truck door, turned to hop out, and turned back and kissed her on the cheek. "I do love you, Ma Poo. I don't know what my mother was like, but I hope she was something like you."

I hopped out of the truck with my donut and closed the door. I didn't look back. I walked away, heading east in my boots with my backpack on. Following the birds.

Chapter 7

I walked straight across a field of mostly dirt and into the woods. I'd acted strong a moment ago, but what I really wanted to do was turn and sprint back to Ma Poo as fast as I could.

Once I was hidden by the brush and trees, I stopped and looked back. The truck was gone and every part of me with it, leaving me empty. I collapsed on the ground on my knees, threw the donut, and cried out. Where would I go? What was I going to do? *I'm a kid. Don't I need someone to look after me?*

I sat there, hugging my knees to my chest, and cried. Minutes felt like hours. What did it matter if I never left that spot? No one knew where I was anyway. "Gramps," I mumbled. "Where are you?"

I didn't know what I was going to do, but I knew Gramps was counting on me. Finally, I dried my eyes. *Are you done now? Get going. You're not going to find the way by sitting in the dirt feeling sorry for yourself. Get up!* I told myself like Gramps would've. It worked. I lifted myself from the ground as if someone was pulling me up and set off in the direction the birds had gone.

...

Midday, the sun was scorching. I walked with beads of sweat rolling down my face and neck, anxious for the next crop of trees. There was a wooded area ahead, but I had to be careful. In this part of Florida, the woods went on forever and could quickly change to marsh. The ground was dry in some areas and wet in others. You wouldn't know you were in a hole until you started sinking, because it was covered with murky water, just like the solid ground.

I'd never been so weary. It was the heat. I took off my jacket and tied it around my waist. My determined steps became a traipse. And just when I thought my legs were too tired to go any further, I came to a clearing, hearing laughter.

Dragonflies zipped by, and I wished Stooby was there to see them. We would've chased them together.

I could hear water splashing and hurried toward the sound. Kids were jumping into a swimming hole. Gramps told me these random holes were once sinkholes. He could've made that up, though, to make me stay away from them. He knew I didn't like sinkholes.

I lowered myself in the tall grass and watched the kids.

"Hey, you! Girl in the stripes!"

"We can see you!"

I stood.

"Are you getting in?"

I shook my head.

"Why not?"

I shrugged.

"Aww... She's scared," said a little boy. "Hey, let's play Marco Polo."

"Get in and cool off. Your shirt's all wet, anyway," another kid said before jumping in.

"Leave her alone. She doesn't have to get in if she doesn't want to," said a girl. "She probably doesn't know how to swim."

"I do."

She climbed out of the hole and into the grass. We were about the same size. As she put on her clothes over her wet bathing suit, I walked closer.

"I should've been smart like you. Our mom didn't say we could get wet. She'd probably say we'd catch something from getting in there. I couldn't help it. It's so hot out, and it's not even summer yet. Plus, we're kids. We can't do everything right. Right?"

"Right," I replied. I was an expert at doing things wrong.

"Come on, T." She turned back to me.

"T?"

"T is for tarantula."

"No, it's not!" he exclaimed while sitting on the ground to put his pants on, not realizing his wet bottom was now covered in dirt. "I'm T because my dad gave me a man's name. I'm not even a man yet."

"His real name is Terrence," said the girl.

"I like T better," I replied.

"Me too," said T.

"I'm Robin."

"Like the bird?"

"Yes. Uh, why are you staring at my hair like that?"

"I'm sorry. I've never seen that in person."

"That? You mean cornrows?"

Robin had what seemed like a hundred tiny cornrows that came together in a ponytail with pretty beads on the ends.

"Yes. I've only seen hair like yours on television." I found myself reaching for her braids without realizing it. "Oh, I'm sorry."

"You can touch them. It's weird, but you do you."

The braids were soft, and there were rubber bands below the beads.

"Did you just sniff her braid?" asked T.

I dropped it quickly. "Sorry."

They both laughed, and Robin looked at my hair. "Your texture is about like mine. I bet my cousin could do yours too."

T walked ahead. "We better get home."

"Which way are you going?" Robin asked.

I pointed.

"Us too. We can walk together. Why are you wearing boots?"

"Because I like them. Plus, I have a long way to go. I may have to walk through water."

"What? Oh, you said walk *through* water. I thought you said walk *on* water."

They laughed. I didn't get it.

"You know, like Jesus."

"Oh, yeah."

They waved at the three kids they left behind. As we walked, Robin talked about her school and needing to finish her homework. It wasn't long before I noticed houses in the distance. Then we came upon some boys with hammers.

"What are they going to do with those?" I asked.

"I'm going to check it out," said T, and we followed.

The boys didn't notice us. "Harder!" one of them said.

The other one raised the hammer and brought it down hard on a tortoise shell.

I grimaced and felt my stomach tighten.

"What's wrong?" asked Robin.

"Why are they doing that?"

"Turtle soup."

"Tastes like beef," said T. "It's really good."

Robin walked away. "Are you coming?"

It took a moment for me to start walking again. I knew people ate frog legs, but that didn't upset me. Turtles were different. They were innocent creatures.

"Don'cha eat meat?" T asked. I guess he knew what I was thinking.

"Not turtles," I said and followed behind all the way to their house.

"We have company!" Robin yelled into the living room.

"Who's this?" asked a teen boy who looked more like her than T did.

"This is uh ...What's your name?"

"What did I tell you about bringing random kids home with you?"

"Ignore my brother. He's an idiot."

"I'm Lou. Luella."

"She's Lou. See? She's not random."

"Piper, can you comb her hair?" she yelled through the house.

How many people live here? I'd already seen about seven people. I was so used to it being just me, Gramps, and Ma Poo, that Robin's family was almost overwhelming.

"Don't be scared. Come on."

I followed her through the house. "That's Dan and that's Piper's mom. My mom is at work."

"Everyone lives here? All of you?"

"No, but all our family have houses on this land, so we're together a lot. My grandfather owned all of the land, and he wanted to make sure his family had their own property. T and I even have a plot for when we grow up and build a house. But I'm moving away when I go to college."

"Why?"

"Because it's a whole big world out there, much bigger than South Florida."

I was surprised. I thought people wanted to stick with their family the way I wanted to stick with Gramps and Ma Poo, not leave them.

"I don't even know what it's like to be alone," she continued.

"Believe me, it's no fun."

"Let me see this head," said a teen girl I figured was Piper. Her hair was braided too—even more elaborate than Robin's. She lifted one of my mangled braids. "What in the world?"

"It got wet."

"Your people let you go around like this?"

"Do I look bad?"

"Do you look bad?" she laughed. "Hmmm. . ."

"What?" asked Robin.

"I'm trying to figure out how much to charge her."

"You got money?" Robin whispered.

I shook my head.

"You can't charge her. You need to do a freebie once in a while."

"No, I don't."

"Consider it like paying tithes or giving to charity. Even big corporations do that."

Robin sure knew about a lot of stuff. But I couldn't figure out why they were so nice. They invited me into their home and now they wanted to do my hair? I'd never gone outside of Osowaw City. Could the whole world be this nice? No, it couldn't. I'd forgotten about the people that were looking for me.

"I should get going."

"It's too late for you to go home. You said you had a long way to go, and the sun is setting. Will your parents be upset if you stay? No point trying to find your way in the dark."

It would be nice to sleep somewhere clean and dry. "Okay."

"Okay, she says," Robin laughed.

"Use the phone in the kitchen to call your mom," said Piper.

I walked in the direction she pointed and looked around. "It's right there," said Robin. "Forget it. Here. I unlocked it."

I stared at the cell phone. I never had a use for one at home. Who would I call? Gramps had one, but he rarely used it. Often, Ma Poo sat out in the cool of the day and I could hear her laughing and knew she was on her phone.

"Don't you know how? I'm not judging. A lot of people don't have cell phones," said Robin.

"On Mars," said T as he chased another boy through the kitchen.

She tapped a green button and the screen switched to numbers. "Just tap the phone number and push that circle. Okay?"

"Okay."

"I'm going to change out of these wet clothes real quick. Be right back."

I watched her walk into the next room. What was I going to do? Minutes passed and I hadn't called anyone. Then Piper passed by, and I tapped the phone, but it was locked again. I faked calling someone and set the phone on the table.

Robin looked up as I walked into the living room. "You can stay?"

"Yes," I replied.

"Yay!" she exclaimed as she hopped up, grabbed my hand, and dragged me from the room. She stopped inside a door and flipped the light switch. I gasped. I couldn't believe my eyes.

"Fairy lights," said Robin.

"It's beautiful. Like a wall of fireflies."

"If you say so. This is my bedroom. You'll sleep over there on that bed."

I went and sat on the pink blanket and rubbed my hand over the flowers.

"Not now, silly. Acting like you've never seen a bed before."

"Never one so pretty."

"Really? Thanks. Let's go outside."

I followed her and everyone smiled or spoke to me as we went to the backyard. *This kind of thing must happen all the time around here. Hello stranger. Yes, come right on in. Welcome to the family.*

...

Robin's family was loud, happy, and went from house to house throughout the evening. It was a merry time, like Christmas every day. Robin said that they all ate dinner together on Sundays.

I sat on one of the steps of the porch, listening to them. Some of the words they spoke were foreign to me. I nodded and grinned when I didn't understand. All the while, I couldn't help but think, *Gramps kept me away from all of this—from the world. Was it on purpose, to hide me?*

At bedtime, I could hear the family in other parts of the house chattering and laughing, and someone outside playing an acoustic guitar. I was happy for them—that they had each other. And as I closed my eyes, I wondered if Gramps was okay. If he had a bed to lie down in, if those people had dogs sniffing around trying to track me, and if Ma Poo had made it north to her family.

I dreamed of Gramps that night. I ran to him in the sunlight. He told me to keep moving, and I promised him I would.

The sun was just peeking through the window when I awoke. It was early enough that the house was silent, except for the occasional snore from

Robin. I sat up and admired her twinkle lights, still on and forming a lit rainbow above her bed.

My hair brushed against my arm. It hung down to my hips. Piper had washed and blown it out. She preferred to braid it after that. Which she was going to do that day before I left.

But I remembered what Gramps said in my dream and tiptoed out of the room and slipped outside.

I looked up at the sky, searching for the birds to show me the way. They were squawking and chirping and flying east. "I see you," I said as I sat on the porch swing, looking out at the neighborhood of houses. Ten in all, neatly spaced apart. This early, they were still and peaceful as if asleep. Soon, they'd come to life.

It wasn't long before I smelled bacon. But I didn't go inside until Robin came looking for me, afraid to just walk back in like I was one of them.

"I've been looking all over for you, Lou. It's time to eat. Then we're going to school."

"School? But—"

She walked away, totally ignoring what I was trying to tell her. I followed her to the kitchen. Bacon, grits, toast, scrambled eggs, and a fruit bowl had been placed on the table.

"What will you have?" Robin's mom asked.

"Everything."

They all laughed.

"Grab a plate," said T, as if I were part of the family. A part of me wished I was. Then I wouldn't have to head God-knows-where to find my people.

"Did you call your mom, Lou?"

"Yes?"

"Where is she?" asked their mother.

"Over at Piper's," said Robin before I could respond.

"Oh, good."

I looked up with my mouth open and full of food.

"Close your mouth," whispered T.

Robin shot me a glance that I knew meant not to disagree.

...

"Let's go," Robin said as soon as we were washed, fed, and my hair was in a long ponytail with one of her headbands.

"Where are we going?"

"I told you. To school, silly."

I looked east. "I—I don't know."

"You can go home after school."

She was right. I could still head that way later. It wouldn't hurt to see what a real school was like, would it?

I followed them down the road. There were two other kids waiting with backpacks.

"I was slick the way I handled that, right?" asked Robin.

"What?"

"When my mom asked where your mom was. I know you didn't really call anyone. People can check their phones. Remember that the next time you fake a call. The way I see it, you're a runaway. Aren't you? I mean, you can tell me. I won't turn you in."

"I'm not. I'm trying to get to my home. I have to find my Gramps too."

"Is it far?" asked T. "Because you're a kid—all by yourself. That's dangerous."

I wished I knew how far it was to Storey, but I had no idea.

A yellow bus pulled up, and they climbed on.

"Come on, Lou. It's not gonna bite ya!" Robin said from the top step. I read the words Watch Your Step on the top stair and did what was asked, holding onto the bar and carefully stepping onto each step. I kept my head down. I didn't look into the faces of the other kids on the bus and sat next to Robin. It pulled off.

"Never been on a bus before, hunh?"

"No." I held tight onto the seat because of the way it bumped along—worse than Gramps's truck. Robin grabbed my hand for a moment, and I relaxed. I smiled to myself as I looked out the window, grateful for a friend. "We're not going east," I said to myself.

"East?"

"The way I'm supposed to go. . ."

"Oh, you can go that way when we get back. Our school has this rule that when you have family in town, they can come to school with you. All you need is a note."

"I don't have a note."

She pulled a piece of paper from her pocket and grinned. "Note."

Chapter 8

The bus stopped in front of a long, white, one-story building, and all the kids stood and climbed off. I followed close behind Robin, keeping pace with everyone else, through the main doors.

"Close your mouth," said T as we walked inside. But I couldn't help it. All the colors and signs and banners had my eyes flashing everywhere. Kids were talking and going their separate ways to their classes. I looked through every window and had the oddest urge to touch everything, even the shiny floor.

"Come on," said Robin, pulling me along. "Before someone determines you're a being from another planet."

We walked down the hall and turned into another entrance. "This is D hall, where my class is. Put your backpack in there."

She turned to a tall woman with a short purple haircut. "Mrs. Qualley, this is my cousin, Luella. She's visiting for today. Here." Robin handed the teacher the note and pulled me over to her desk. "Sit there," she said of the desk beside hers.

For once, I felt like everyone else. Just a kid in class for the day instead of being homeschooled, often outside at our picnic table. But I also missed the way my life with Gramps was.

"Class," said Mrs. Qualley. "We have a visitor today. Luella, please tell us where you're from."

I felt everyone's eyes on me.

"Luella? What kind of name is Luella?" said the boy in front of me with a frown.

"I know this one," said Mrs. Qualley. "It has variants: Lu, Lulu, Lula. . ." she said as she wrote my name on the board.

"It's a thing she does. All the time," Robin whispered.

Mrs. Qualley continued, "It means famous warrior and light."

I grinned.

She went to a book on her desk and thumbed through the pages. "Here it is. It also means famous elf." She grinned. "Which are you? A famous warrior of a famous elf?"

Everyone laughed.

I didn't know what to say, so I shrugged. Elf wasn't a word Gramps used. Ma Poo did during Christmas. But it wasn't a part of my studies.

The day progressed on. Since I wasn't really a student, I didn't have to do the work, participate, or get called on by the teacher. Gramps had done a good job. I understood all of the math. I sat quietly with my hands folded in front of me on the desk. That's how I thought all good students sat in school.

Mrs. Qualley began a lesson on swamps and talked about the various plants, trees, and wildlife. "It's best to keep yourself covered up because of the mosquitoes and chiggers in the tall grasses."

I raised my hand like I'd seen everyone else do.

"What are you doing? Put your hand down," Robin whispered.

I thought the class needed to hear from someone who actually lived on a swamp, so I raised it higher. Robin pulled my hand down, and I raised it again.

"Would you like to say something, Luella?"

"Yes."

"Go ahead."

All the kids turned to listen.

"There are no-see-ums, too. The females have to have a meal before they lay eggs."

"What's the meal?" asked the boy in front of me.

"Us. Like a mosquito bite. And they're so small, they fit through your screen door. Swamps aren't all bad, though. I mean, there's gators and snakes, and don't be fooled, gators climb fences."

"They do?" asked the boy.

"Yes, because my house has a creek on one end and a lake on the other. And we have lots of swamp stuff going on. And the birds—"

"How do you keep the gators out?" a girl asked.

"I tell them not to come near our house."

"I've heard it all. This girl said she talks to gators," another kid said with a laugh.

Why was that funny?

Robin sat with her hand over her eyes.

"Settle down, everyone," said Mrs. Qualley. "Thank you for sharing, Luella."

I smiled, but I was a little embarrassed about saying anything further.

At lunchtime, Mrs. Qualley came over to our desks. "Robin, your letter says Luella is from Georgia. What she described doesn't sound like Georgia to me."

"You don't know there are swamps in Georgia?" I asked. "But you're a teacher."

"Oh." She looked surprised. "I don't know why I was thinking Atlanta."

"Good save," Robin whispered. "Let's go eat."

Our class entered the cafeteria, and I followed Robin to the lunch line. I wore a badge with my name, and I guess it also gave me access to food. "Do what I do," Robin instructed.

I grabbed a tray and reached for a red and white carton of milk. "Get chocolate. It's better," she instructed and pointed to the right at the brown and white cartons. We moved right down the line with everyone else. A cheeseburger and fries, peas, a fruit cup, and a chocolate pudding were placed on my tray.

"Don't look so happy," Robin said. I immediately frowned.

We sat at a table with some other girls. I watched them open their milk and then copied them. Only, they didn't spill any. I unwrapped my plastic spoon. "Girl, if you go for those peas, I will disown you," said Robin.

I stopped mid shovel.

"No one eats the peas. It makes you look weird."

"Peas are good for you," I said as I picked up one.

"Don't you dare."

I popped it in my mouth and crossed my eyes.

Instead of disowning me, she couldn't stop laughing.

"Swamp girl," said a boy passing by with his tray.

"Shut up, Benjamin," Robin spewed. "Don't make me do what happened last time. And you know what happened last time."

He walked away silently.

"What happened last time?"

"T and I got him after school."

"What did you get him?"

She laughed again. "We caught a bunch of geckos and put them in his shirt."

I giggled. "Once I scared Gramps with a gecko. Then I tried to catch it, and its tail fell off."

After lunch we had recess. It was fun. Then in gym class, someone kept calling me an overachiever. I smiled, unsure if that was a compliment or an insult.

The school library was a whole lot bigger than the one at Osowaw City Hall. They had more than one computer, and they were newer models.

Robin pulled me over to them. "Let's find your home." She turned on the monitor and began to type. "Well? Where do you live?"

I thought about what happened the last time. If she typed in Storey, would those people appear here at the school?

"I'm from Osowaw City."

Her hands dropped from the keyboard. "You're from Osowaw City? No one lives there."

"Yes, we do. There are kids too."

"There are?"

"Yes. It's small, but downtown is a whole block long."

She shook her head. "No one lives there. It's all woods. But that explains a lot."

When we left the school that day, I said goodbye to everyone and was sure to miss Mrs. Qualley, and even Benjamin.

I don't think I ever laughed as much as I did with Robin. All the way back down the lane to her house. "You two sure look to've had a good day," said Piper. "I can finish your hair now, Lou."

"Maybe later," I replied.

"Later, meaning you're going to stay awhile longer?" asked Robin, excited.

"Just a little longer." I grinned.

"Yay! Water soakers," Robing exclaimed.

"Don't you dare get her hair wet," said Piper.

"Oh, yeah. I forgot."

Sometime around dinner, everyone was outside. I was back by Piper's house, playing catch with T, when I saw cars pulling onto the road. They stopped next to one of Robin's uncles at the entrance walking his dog. He talked to the driver of the first car, then nodded and pointed toward the houses.

"Lou, let's go inside," Robin said as she ran to me.

"We're playing," said T.

"Play later."

We went in through the back door and peeked out the window.

The cars pulled up between Robin's and Piper's houses.

"We're looking for a little girl. Has anyone seen her?" asked a man wearing a black suit.

"There are a lot of kids around here, mister."

The man held up a photo.

"I don't recognize her," said T.

"You mind if we look around?"

"Not without a warrant," said Robin's uncle.

"We'll just talk to your neighbors. Maybe one of them has seen something."

"That's all of us here. We're all one family and we own all of these houses."

"Oh. Well, still."

Robin was pulling me now, but I wanted to hear what they were saying. She grabbed my arm and backpack and shoved me into the pantry. "I'll be back."

I waited, but feared I'd miss too much of what was said. No one was in the house when I stepped out of the closet and watched from the window.

"This is a private road you're on, and I'm going to have to ask you to leave," said another member of the family. "We don't take kindly to strangers around here. Now, you can leave a card or something and we'll let you know if we see a little girl. Although, what would you want with a little girl?"

The men didn't seem as big and bad as the ones that came to my house. They were dressed the same, but they didn't look like they wanted to cross Robin's family.

I backed away, out the back door, and around the back side of the house. I was well beyond their property when I heard someone running. I turned and waited for Robin.

"Why'd you leave? We had your back."

"It's time that I go. I stayed too long. I hope I can see you again someday."

Robin hugged me. T caught up to us and hugged me too. Then Robin handed me her lunch bag. "There are snacks in there, those biscuits you liked, and water. Why are those people—"

"They're really bad. They took my grandfather."

"The one you're looking for?"

I nodded.

"Why are they looking for you?" asked T.

"Because of where I come from."

"The swamp?"

I wanted to tell her more, but I couldn't. Her family had made me forget about Storey for a moment—made me believe I was like them. I even began to feel I fit in. But these weren't my people. I had to get to them.

"Thanks for my hair."

"Do not let it get back the way it was or I'll—"

"Disown me, right?"

We both laughed.

"Friends forever?" asked Robin.

"You bet."

They watched me walk away.

"How do you know the way?" Robin called after me.

"The birds."

Chapter 9

I walked until nightfall and didn't see another soul. But I wasn't lonely, because I talked to everything I saw—gnats, grasshoppers, crows. I kept heading east and didn't so much as eat a thing until I stopped under a huge oak tree.

"You're an old one," I said as I placed my hand on the bark. "Protect me tonight and shield me from the rain." It was coming. I could smell it.

I sat at the base of the oak and listened as its leaves closed over me, forming a canopy. I ate two of the maple biscuits and drank half of the bottled water, braided my ponytail into a long braid, and leaned back against the tree.

"Everything, stay twenty feet away." That meant bugs, animals, everything. I watched a few fireflies twinkle in the distance, reminding me of Robin's bedroom wall. Then the rain came, and just as I asked, the oak shielded me. Not a drop of water came through its leaves.

When I awoke, I was curled in a ball on my side, using my backpack as a pillow. My jacket covered me like a blanket. A few sun rays passed through the openings between trees. I'd had a good rest, even though the frogs had become especially noisy. "Mating season," Gramps used to say.

I stood, brushed myself off, and placed my hand against the big oak. "Thank you. You are just as majestic as you appear." The leaves spread out again, removing the canopy.

I looked up, listening for the chirping and squawking of the birds. "Which way?" I asked. They flitted in the trees and flew off all at once. I followed.

No matter how far I walked, I never came across anything letting me know Storey was near. I expected to see a great palace rise in the distance. That's what I hoped for, anyway.

I was running alongside a river when I saw something climbing from the bank. It was soaking wet and big like a dog. The hair, wet and flat, made it look strange. *That's an awful large raccoon,* I thought. Then it stopped and reared its pointed teeth.

I froze, staring into its eyes as it faced me. "Just keep walking. Go where you're going. Go on."

It slowly continued on. I wasn't used to seeing them when the sun was so high. Gramps and I could always hear their short howl-yips when they called to their packs at dawn or dusk, letting them know their location.

"They're just boys in the hood," Gramps had jokingly told me once. I laughed until I could do nothing but lie on the floor holding my stomach.

"Leave'em be, and they'll leave you be."

"Why do we need them?" I'd asked.

"They play an ecological role."

"Ecological?"

"I hadn't planned for this to be part of your lesson today, but what would happen if we had too many skunks and raccoons?" he'd asked.

"That wouldn't be good."

"Right. Coyotes help maintain balance. We're good, as long as they stay away from here." We didn't have any animals, so there was no 'good eating' for them. But Gramps helped Ma Poo put a six-foot fence around the coop with little boxes attached, powered by the sun, that kept animals out.

I didn't move until the coyote was good and gone. I didn't take any roads but traveled through fields and woods and kept heading east. The birds were not always flying. But I stayed my course.

"You there!"

I spun around. *Me?*

"What are you doing out here in the middle of nowhere?" asked the woman.

"What are *you* doing out here?"

"Don't sass me."

"I'm not. I'm just asking," I said as she neared me. Gramps had told me about people who didn't have a home. Not like me, but people who lived on the streets like in the movies I watched with Ma Poo. The without-a-home people. No, the word was homeless.

A dog barked in the distance.

"You get over here, Boris," she called.

Boris?

"That dog ain't worth two dead flies." She sucked her teeth. "I don't know what you're doing back here, but it ain't safe."

"*You're* here."

"I live here. But it ain't for everybody. It's hard living, but then I'm not a soft person. C'mo," she said as she turned.

C'mo?

"This way!"

I followed her, listening to something clang as she walked. Through some trees, a clearing, and more trees, was a shack—barely large enough to be called a house. Though she touted proudly, "That's my place right there."

To me, it looked like a good sneeze might blow it down. I thought of the story of the three little pigs just as I noticed pigs in the fenced area beside it. She took a pail from under the huge coat she wore in the ninety-degree weather and dumped it in there. The pigs went to eating.

"Hungry? I cooked up some rabbit."

I looked around. Could I possibly have gone back in time? "No. Thank you. I'll be going on my way now."

"Sit a spell. I don't get many folks out here."

"What is this place?"

She squatted like she was sitting on something. "Best I can tell, someone lived here a long time ago. I found it. Took it over and made it what it is now. What's your name?"

"Lou."

"Lou?"

"Luella. What's yours?"

"Finch."

"Like the bird?"

"You got that right. My last name, but that's what I go by. Your folks know where you are?"

"Yes," I lied.

"Umm-hmm... Boris!"

The dog came running.

"Where did you go, you crazy dog. This here's Lou. You be nice to her, ya hear?"

Boris walked over to me so I could pet him. *Did he understand her like animals understand me? Is she like me?* A grin covered my face.

"Hey, girl..."

"Lou," I said as I petted Boris.

"What you got in that bag? Let me see."

My smile disappeared. I thought I was beginning to like her, but she was pushy and reached for Robin's lunch bag, snatching it before I could pull it away. She opened the granola bar, ate it, and then drank the rest of my water. Then she burped.

"What else you got?" she asked as she picked her teeth.

"I'm leaving now."

"Oh, don't go off all half-cocked. I don't mean no harm. Alone too much is all. Out of touch with everyone else."

I knew that feeling. And for a moment, she seemed sad. Then she was off to her crazy self again, hopping up and running after Boris.

My old life with Gramps and Ma Poo was looking better and better.

After a few minutes, she ran back to me, breathing heavily. "So are you lost or what? Do you know the way home?"

She was too close now, and I had to cover my nose for the stench.

"I was told to follow the birds."

"Birds? More likely the rats." She snickered. "I bet there's a reward for bringing you home. You think? Maybe I should go with you. Come here," she said as she grabbed me. Her hand was rough and callused. And hot.

"Let me go."

"What's in that backpack?"

"Nothing. Stop!"

She pulled in one direction, and I pulled in the other. I knew I was strong, but she was dragging me, and I wasn't letting go. She wrenched backward toward her shack.

"Let go!"

Boris kept barking. I didn't know if it was at me or her.

I could feel heat building in my chest. My emotions were ready to explode. She kept pulling, but at the same time, she was tiring too. Gramps always said I was strong and mostly muscle, so I held on with all my might. Then she yanked the bag up high and quickly turned it hard to the left. I fell over and landed against a log.

The most wicked-sounding laugh came from her as she hugged the bag to her chest and backed inside the house.

I scrambled toward her, and she slammed the door.

"Please give it back. Please," I said as I banged on the shed. There weren't even any windows. What if it rained? My jacket was in there. I didn't even know what Ma Poo had put in the backpack. And then...

I suddenly remembered Gramps's watch. *Oh no!*

"Give it back," I yelled. My chest heaved. I backed away from the house, letting my emotions loose.

The wind picked up.

Boris whimpered and ran away.

"Give it back!" I yelled again, giving her another chance to do the right thing.

The shed began to shake, the wood planks were pulling away from the wall. It was enough. She should've opened the door, but she didn't. I'd given her a chance. Why didn't she give up? Why couldn't she have listened to me? What happened next wasn't my fault.

The shed exploded.

Finch lay on the floor, holding the backpack. I ran up and snatched it from her. I didn't know if anything had been inside the shed but if anything had, it was gone now—blown to bits. *Good luck finding a place to sleep.*

I backed away. I wouldn't take my eyes off such a sneaky person even for a moment.

She rose on her side and slumped onto her elbow.

"They know you know the way. They're not stupid. Let'em in. It benefits both worlds. They're going to find you, you know."

I'd finally turned away but looked back over my shoulder. "Let them try."

...

I could only assume whoever those people were, they were going to pay Finch to keep me there or turn me in. I had so many questions. How did they know I would go that way? How did they know I was out there at all? Why would she want my backpack? She said they knew I knew the way, but I didn't.

I saw a movie once with Ma Poo, before she covered my eyes. She said she didn't want me seeing what was going to happen to the woman because I'd see it in my dreams. "Have to be careful of what we let in," she'd said.

The woman was being tortured for information. Would they do that to Gramps?

They didn't come after us because we're from Storey. From what Finch said, what they really wanted to know was the way to Storey.

As I walked, I thought about everything Gramps ever told me about the place we're from. How grand everything was, how amazing the foods were, how the clothes were different, and the smell of blossoms that were not like any flower I'd ever known. I wanted to be there. But I wanted to be there with him. I had no way to find him, so I had no choice but to keep going.

I never stopped for anyone else, not that I saw anyone else. If I thought I heard someone, I hid, only to find it was a deer, a bobcat, or a wild pig.

When I awoke the next morning, I could instantly tell something was wrong. The forest was oddly silent, other than the rumbling of my stomach.

"Show me the way," I said as I sat up.

Nothing happened.

I stepped out from beneath the oak tree that had shielded me for the night. "Show me," I said in a whisper, feeling what my mind didn't want to accept. "Come on... Please. Take to the sky."

It was no use. The birds were gone. All of them. There was not one cheep or chirp.

"But that's impossible." *The birds just disappeared? All the birds in Florida? That can't happen.* Yet they didn't respond when I called. *Did something take the birds? How?* I suddenly remembered that day when we were all together sitting at the picnic table having an early supper. Gramps and I had looked out into the distance, both of us looking over the swamp land beyond the property at the same time.

"It's getting closer," Gramps said. But he wouldn't tell me what he meant.

What did I see?

I squeezed my eyes shut trying to remember. It was a flash, like light escaping a cloud. Quick. Not even a second. Whatever that was had taken the birds so I couldn't find my way. I leaned back against the tree. Now I'd never get home. I could turn back and try to get to Robin's house, but I'd promised Gramps. He made me promise, because he knew I wasn't so good at following directions. I couldn't let him down.

My stomach growled. I took everything out of the backpack to see what I had. I don't know why I didn't do that in the first place. *Jerky. Thank you, Ma Poo.* Crackers, a juice box, socks. *What's this?* I unfolded the paper. *It's a map. But how is this useful if I don't know where I am?* I couldn't find Storey anywhere on it.

I was frustrated. "How am I supposed to get to Storey now?" I groaned.

Light emitted from the backpack. *Finch didn't take it?* I stuck my hand in the tiny side pocket and pulled out the pocket watch. This time I opened it. I noticed an edge on the outer lip had lifted. I dug my nail beneath it. That part clicked and opened, revealing it wasn't a watch at all, but a compass. And where the N should've been for north was. . . STOREY.

Chapter 10

I studied the compass for a while, flipping it back and forth in my hand. Was it just a label or would it lead me to Storey? The Earth has a magnetic field. It's a huge magnet. That's what Gramps taught me in my science lessons. That's how compasses work. He said to hold a compass flat and to make sure the direction-of-travel arrow pointed in the direction you wanted to go. But what direction was that?

I pointed the compass around, expecting the dial to spin or something. But nothing happened. The chain hung below it. I lifted it over my head. I figured it was best to keep it on me. No matter how I pointed it, the needle didn't move.

"You're not glowing anymore, either" I told it. Then, I had an idea. I gathered all my things into the backpack and put it on, took a deep breath, and counted. *One. Two. Three.* Based on the compass shining so brightly whenever I said "Storey", I didn't know what would happen when I said the name while having it out in the open.

"Storey!" I shouted.

The light was bright, but not as bright as before. Maybe because it was daylight out. The dial spun, and then stopped at an angle to my right. I jumped around excitedly and pointed. "That way?" My body shot forward.

"Whoa! Wait!" Only having been a couple of feet above the ground, I landed and rolled into a bush. "No way," I said as I stood and looked back.

The best I figured, I was a hundred feet from where I'd been standing.

"What is this thing?" I thought for a moment. I wasn't sure that was the way I wanted to travel. At least, not until I had to cross an open area or over a marsh. Those areas were always waterlogged. They're all grass and no trees—nowhere for me to hide if those people found me. So I'd need to get across as quickly as possible.

I walked in the direction the compass had tried to shoot me and got excited. *Could this be it? Could it happen today? I'll actually reach Storey?*

I came upon a mudflat, and beyond that was a marsh filled with brown, furry spiked cattails and maidencane. I readied myself.

"Storey!" I screamed again as I held out the compass as if I were passing it to someone. I darted across the marsh and looked down over the lake it connected to. In no time, I was across and passing through a wooded area. Branches snapped from the force of my flight. I was afraid to close my eyes and afraid not to, for fear I'd ram into a tree. But I didn't want to stop. I wanted to hurry and get to Storey.

As I flew out of the woods, I crossed over a roadway. The passengers in the vehicles looked up at me as I passed. Was I just a glimmer to them, or could they see me—covered in dirt, my long thick ponytail flying, backpack on, looking down at them?

Once I entered the next patch of trees, I stopped. I stayed low and watched the caravan of cars. They'd stopped too.

"They saw me."

An SUV turned into the field. *They're everywhere. Were they searching every road in the state? Did they see the compass?* I lifted it from my chest. "Can you tell me how far I am?"

I expected it to speak or give me some clue. No such luck.

I fell to my knees and lowered my head. I touched the ground, hoping whatever was in me that gave me this ability would radiate through the roots of the trees and every living thing. "If anything tries to take me away, you protect me. Don't let it happen, got it? Thank you."

Now the earth, I could hear. Not in words. I could feel the voice of the trees. We were in solidarity. "Good, good. . ." I whispered as I stood and receded into the woods.

As I walked, I thought things out. I still had not noticed a sign of any bird, as if they never existed. No herons or cranes. Not even a scrub-jay. I had no way of contacting Gramps or Ma Poo, and the evil people were looking for me everywhere. I didn't know who they were, only that they wore black and wanted to get to Storey. But why were they looking for *me*? Gramps was from Storey too, but they were more interested in me. I had to find a way to save him, but how could I if I couldn't save myself?

I sat for a while, so still that anyone passing by would've missed me. The sun was setting. The woods quickly darkened.

"I see you," I said as I watched it walk by. "You're not hopping, and you don't have a fluffy tail. You're a marsh rabbit, aren't you?" It glanced at me. "What do you know, little rabbit? What have you seen around here? Are you alone too? Tell me about this place."

It disappeared beneath a thicket.

...

The next morning, there was no sign of any birds. I even listened for the hoot of an owl the night before. They were my alarm clock and my music. They were my guides. Now, nothing.

I started my journey again. For the first time in my life, I wished for a bath before someone could tell me to take one. Beyond the forest, I walked beside a ditch alongside a train track and came upon a rickety trestle bridge. It crossed over a stream. I stepped up to it. The tracks were rusted, and the slats beneath them were gray and looked as if they would split.

Standing on the tracks, I found myself looking straight down at the stream. The next two slats were missing, and the one after that had a black hole as if someone had lit a fire on it. *Way out here? In the middle of nowhere?* To the left of the track was another track, but it was in even worse condition. "Worse for wear," Gramps would've said.

Swimming across the stream would've been my first choice, but I had to keep my backpack and the compass dry. I stretched my leg forward onto the burned slat and tapped it with my foot. It was solid enough. I hopped to the next one and kept going until I was at the center of the bridge. I looked out over the creek.

It was a beautiful, peaceful sight, watching the water flow gently away. Gramps would've loved it. I could see him in his fishing hat, three fishing rods in hand with his rusted tackle box on the ground, casting his lines off the bridge. Me beside him, watching a white heron take flight from the buttonwoods and cabbage palms.

I screamed his name, as though he'd hear me and come running. Not Leon, but his name from

Storey. K'Awil-Philokalia. He told me it a long time ago, but he said never to repeat it. I could barely pronounce it, let alone repeat it. But I remembered his Storey name because it sounded magical.

I missed Gramps terribly. Not just his love. His frustration too. When I didn't take my lessons seriously or didn't do my chores. When I'd take his duck caller and go about harassing the ducks on the lake. When I'd test how close I could get to a gator, inching closer and closer so I could see how fast I could get away. When I'd hear him calling me and hide so I could hop out and scare him. It rarely worked, but I laughed hysterically. I know he enjoyed my games, although he'd never say it. What he'd say was, "Great day, Lou. It's never a dull moment round here."

Then there was the time I dipped my hand in the lake and told the fish to jump into the boat. They started flying in from every direction and flopping around all over the place. There were so many, they almost sunk us. I was much younger then. A few of them almost knocked us out too. Gramps looked shocked, and not in a good way. He was disappointed in me.

"You need to understand the value in accomplishing something—working for what you have, even though you don't have to," he'd said. I missed those moments.

As I stood looking out over the water, I glanced down, feeling the bridge vibrating under my feet. And it wasn't my emotions this time. But I was so distraught, I didn't move. I watched the train approach the bridge. *Go! Get off the bridge. Get to Storey,* I told myself.

Finally, I ran, jumping the slats. The train came up fast. It was right behind me. At the last minute, I jumped.

I flew too far, as the wind from the train brushed past me. I grasped at a floor beam of the second track.

The train whizzed by as I hung there, my feet dangling in the air. It hurt and I strained to lift my legs and wrap them around a beam. I pulled myself up and sat there a moment, catching my breath, one leg on either side of the beam, hanging through the track. *That was a close one.* I hurried the rest of the way across the bridge before another train could come.

I breathed heavily. The air was thick, no longer cooling down at the end of the day like it did in the winter. Although in Florida, we were lucky to have three days of actual winter temperatures. My t-shirt stuck to me. I needed water. Instead of hunkering down for the night, I walked on, hoping to come upon someone who would take pity on a kid and give me something to drink.

I came upon a farm. There were lights on inside the house. I stood outside the fence a moment, listening, waiting for a vibe that this wasn't a good idea, but I didn't get one. I tucked the compass inside my shirt. The metal was cold against my chest. Every few steps, I stopped and looked around. When I got to the house, I snuck around it and found a spigot under one of the windows. *Water! Yes!*

I turned it, rinsed my hands, and then put my palms together to catch the water and drank some. It felt like the sides of my throat had been stuck together and the water unglued it. I splashed some over my face, and then kept scooping and drinking until I realized someone was behind me. I was as still as a squirrel waiting to see if you're a threat before it dashes off.

"Ahem."

My hands dropped, and I slowly stood and turned around. Water ran down my chin onto my wet-with-sweat shirt.

"What are you, a night nymph?" asked the boy. "I don't see any wings, so maybe not."

I stared at him.

"*¿Hablas inglés? ¿Estás bien?*"

"I was thirsty," I said while wiping my mouth on my arm. I recognized the boy was carrying a BB gun on his shoulder similar to Ronnie's.

"I can see that," he replied. "My dad sent me out here. You know from inside the house, we can hear if you turn on the water outside. Something shakes in the wall. Just so you know."

"Anything out there, Wren?" a man's voice asked.

"*¡No, Papi!* Maybe it was a black bear!"

"Black bear?" I asked.

"Yeah, we see 'em from time to time." He eyed me. "Where did you come from? There isn't another farm for miles. I think we better call the police."

"No, please, don't."

He looked to be thinking about it. "Maybe you should follow me. I mean, unless you want my dad to come out and see you." He turned and walked away.

I followed him at a distance and waited while he opened the door of a barn. He walked inside and switched on a light. "You're my age. Why are you out wandering around at night?"

He took off his cap and thick wavy hair flowed down around his shoulders.

"You're a girl?"

"Did you think Wren was a boy's name? My mom calls me a songbird. She said I came out of the womb singing. That's why she named me Wren. *El chochín*."

"Like the bird."

"Yes.

"Did someone abandon you?" Her eyes were wide. "Were you kidnapped and in the trunk of someone's car and when they stopped at a gas station, you got away?"

"Did you just make that up?"

She laughed. "I spend a lot of time by myself, so I imagine a lot of stuff."

"Me too."

"It's hot, but you can hide out here if you want. It's better than being outside."

"I don't mind nature."

"Well, the mob can find you easy outside."

"Mob?"

"Saw it in a movie. I'll be right back. Don't move."

A few minutes later the barn door opened again. "Sheesh, you didn't really stand right there the whole time, did ya?"

"What else would I do?"

"*Es muy raro*," she mumbled.

"What?"

"So weird. Here."

She handed me a damp, warm towel. I stared at it, and then at her.

"Don't you want to clean yourself up before you eat?"

"Eat?"

She sat. "Yeah, I brought food."

I wiped the towel over my face and neck and then the few rust stains still on my hands from the bridge. I almost felt bad handing the dirty towel back to her.

"Wow, I didn't think you were *that* dirty."

"I need a bath."

"You think? So here's what I brought. My mom was watching TV, and it's my turn to clean the kitchen so it was easy to sneak some out. I've got cornbread, and there's some field peas and rice in that container. You like sweet tea? Brought you some of that in that thermos too."

I dug into the cornbread first.

"My mom makes the best cornbread," she said as if she were singing. "She uses creamed corn in it."

She sat there, watching me eat. Then, out of nowhere, as if she'd been in my head, she said, "Do you know what's weird? The birds are gone, and now you're here."

"You noticed it too?" I asked with my mouth full.

"I don't think my parents have. I usually hear them in the mornings, and we have suet feeders out back. This time of year, we get visits from red-bellied woodpeckers."

"Are their bellies really red?"

"Hardly. They have red on their heads though. Hey, I once saw a red-cockaded woodpecker and they're endangered!"

"You know a lot about woodpeckers."

"Yeah. It's my hobby. Can you draw? I draw them too."

"I'm not good at art, but I like to paint."

"I bet your paintings are good. What you think is terrible may be a work of art. 'Beauty is in the eye of the beholder,' my dad says. I probably should go before he starts looking for me."

"I should go too."

"But you can sleep in here. At least wait until morning. I'll bring you breakfast." She gave me the blanket she'd been sitting on. "You just stay right there, and don't you move, okay? I'll be back at first light, okay? Don't go anywhere."

She closed the door, and then opened it again. "You can move around the barn, just don't leave it, understand? I don't want to come back and find you in the same spot again."

…

I awoke, looking up at Wren. She shook me.

"All right, I'm up."

"Hurry, you've gotta go. They'll be here soon."

"Who?"

She ran to the barn door, looked out, and came back, gathering my things. "My father called them. They came a few days ago with a picture of you. Something about you being ill?"

"I'm not sick."

"I can tell. You're as fit as a horse. You have the appetite of one too. Hurry up. Get your boots on."

The barn door opened, and we both jumped. "*Ven acá*, Wren," said her father.

She walked toward him as he came closer. "*¡Papi!* She's not sick. They lied."

"Are you okay?" he asked.

I backed away.

"I'm not going to hurt you."

"Then let me go."

"You're free to leave."

That's what he said, but he lunged toward me and caught hold of the chain of the compass. He snatched it off. Wren pulled at his free arm as I fell back and scrambled for my backpack. I ran out the other door on the other side of the barn as fast as I could, clasping my backpack to my chest.

I heard Wren's father when he came after me, and I peered down at him over a thick patch of Spanish moss that draped over him from an oak tree, when he gave up. Had I had the compass, I could've called Storey and zipped out of there.

Now, I had no way of knowing if I was still heading in the right direction.

Before I could climb down from the tree, I heard their engines. I waited there, watching clouds of dirt shooting up from the tires of the approaching vehicles.

Chapter 11

I climbed down from the tree and ran, determined to get as far away from Wren's farm as I could. After a while, I stopped just long enough to place my hand on the ground, reminding the living things of the woods, "Protect me." Then I continued on.

It wasn't long before I sensed I wasn't alone. Just like when I knew that cottonmouth was in my house—how I felt it long before I heard it slither across the floor.

I closed my eyes, feeling something foreign to the woods, and it was all around me. And there were no birds to squawk or shoot away from tree limbs to alert me of where it was.

I ran again. How I wished I still had the compass to zip me out of there. Something whizzed past. Ahead of me, it tore away part of a tree.

I gasped in horror, but I didn't stop. *What was that?* I looked back, seeing a man running to catch me. *Are they firing at me?* Another man was in front running toward me. *I thought they wanted me alive to show them the way to Storey.*

Gramps believed in me. He said I'd make it to Storey. He was sure of it. I had to get away. I slowed, trying to determine my next move. Climbing a tree wouldn't help. More men were approaching behind the others.

I ducked to the right just as something zipped past my ear. I could feel my emotions building and about to explode.

"Okay, take it easy. No one is going to hurt you."

I turned. There was a man on every side now. They talked to each other as if I wasn't there. "We've been out here all night. Let's get this over with."

The ground began to shake.

"Do it before she does something!" the man behind me said.

My heart was beating so fast—too fast.

They all stepped closer at the same time. As soon as I looked away from one of them, I felt something prick my skin. *Run*, I told myself. But it was too late. I couldn't. My body wouldn't listen. I wobbled forward, and then collapsed. My legs wouldn't move, and I couldn't lift up on my arms.

"Got her!" I heard a male voice say.

I don't remember what happened next. I only saw glimpses of things. Men yelling or screaming, I wasn't sure. And Cats. Gigantic cats. Then seeing the sky—moving, and the ground beneath me gliding away. Then everything went black.

When I opened my eyes again, I lay against warm tan fur. I sat up and looked at the lithe animal and its white belly.

What I'd seen weren't cats at all, but Florida panthers. I pulled at my torn hoodie and examined the bruise on my throbbing shoulder.

"You dragged me away, didn't you?" They'd protected me just like I'd asked. "Thank you," I told them.

The largest one neared me with piercing yellow eyes and lowered its head. Then they walked away, all of them going their separate ways.

I felt my chest, just remembering the compass was gone.

...

After watching the panthers leave, I dusted myself off and stood. I didn't know which way to go. Who knows where the panthers dragged me? I looked up at the sun. "The sun rises in the east," Gramps had said. As far as I could tell, by the position of the sun, it was afternoon. I remembered my lesson with Gramps. "The sun isn't moving, we are." That wasn't useful information right now. "If the sun is setting in the west, I need to go in the opposite direction to head east." I wasn't certain I worked that out right, but that's the way I went.

Just before sunset, I smelled salt water. Was I getting closer to the coast? I climbed a tree but could only see marsh in the distance and sporadic woody areas. I stayed in the tree a while. Just as the sun dipped below the horizon, I decided to climb down. Maybe I could walk a little further before resting for the night. Maybe I'd come across someone with food.

No sooner than I leaned over the branch and placed my foot on the one below it, I felt their presence. They hadn't come into view, and I couldn't hear them yet. I climbed back up and waited. Plumes of dark smoke rose from three areas around me. *They're setting the woods on fire?*

The roots of various plant life cried out to me. What was I supposed to do? I had no water. I closed my eyes, spread my arms out wide, and slammed my palms together. I had to grab hold of the tree for the wall of wind that knocked the breath out of me. It smothered the fires, and I breathed in air as if I'd just come up from a deep ocean. I sat on the branch, breathing heavily and regaining my strength.

The sky darkened, and I noticed beams from flashlights. Soon those disappeared.

"Come out," a voice said.

How do they know I'm here?

Behind me, something flew near. *Is that a robot?*

"Luella, we know you're here," a woman's voice said. It was amplified as if coming from a speaker.

I stayed silent. They'd have to climb the tree and get me. I wasn't moving.

"We've brought company. We have friends of yours. And your grandfather, or 'Gramps' as you so affectionately call him. He would love to see you."

They came into view, the woman leading the way and people following her. She pushed Gramps forward. "He's right here. Come to us without releasing your power or calling on something to help you. We won't hurt you; we only want to talk. I promise, no harm will come to your grandfather."

They looked all around them, trying to figure out where I was. I adjusted myself, trying to see Gramps's face so I could determine if he was really okay.

He looked around for me. There was no signal from him or anything to tell me what to do.

"We knew you were here when you didn't let the forest burn. It *was* you, wasn't it? Let me guess, your grandfather taught you everything is connected, right? The plants and animals? You can feel them, can't you?"

"What did you do with the birds?" I yelled.

"She's in the trees," said one of the men.

"The birds are fine. We used a machine that repels them. They can't stand the signal it sends out. As soon as we turn it off, the birds will come back."

I was relieved and eased down the tree. "What do you want?" I asked as I came into view.

"Luella, can you see us?"

"Yes."

She grinned. "Your people amaze me. Here we have to wear night-vision goggles when you can naturally see us clearly in the dark."

She took her goggles off and instructed everyone else to do the same. They switched on lights that shined in an arc around them.

The woman stepped forward. She was older. Almost too old to be out there. Her hair was white and pulled tightly away from her face. "What I want is to go back to Storey. That's all I want."

"You've been there?" I asked.

"Yes, and after they cut ties with Earth, only your family was left with a way to get back."

"No. We were only to see that the gate never reopened. Everything that you've done—this evil and no concern for lives—this is not our way. This is why you can never see Storey again," said Gramps.

A man hit the back of his head, and he fell forward.

"Gramps! Please, don't hurt him." I felt my emotions building quicker than usual, and everything around us began to shake.

The woman held a hand up for them to stop. "Calm down, Luella. I apologize for that. He did not have my permission to do that. Don't hold it against me." She took another step toward me.

The ground continued to shake. The woman shook her head. "My, my ...I'd forgotten the way those from Storey can manipulate gravity. Luella, we must come to an agreement. I don't want any harm to come to your Gramps or your friends."

"What friends?"

Men pushed them forward—Robin, Finch falling on her hands, and Wren. Robin and Wren's eyes were wide. Finch looked as if she were enjoying the whole thing.

I pointed at Finch. "Do what you want to her. She is not my friend."

"Aww... Come on, Lou," said Finch.

"You are a whole lot of crazy," Robin told Finch. "Don't do it, Lou!" That's all she could say before a gloved hand covered her mouth.

The woman spoke again. "Luella, listen to me. We don't want to hurt anyone, but we will. All the violence can end right here. It's up to you. Your grandfather is old—"

"You're old."

"But he doesn't understand. Things are not as simple as they used to be. There are some very important people that will not like it if I come back empty handed."

"Too bad."

"I'm trying to reason with you."

"With weapons pointed at me and that thing flying around?"

"Bring the drones in. Lower your weapons," she told the men.

"But—" one of them protested.

"Lower them," she demanded. "Don't make me tell you again."

The men slowly put their weapons away.

"How am I supposed to get you to Storey?" I asked.

"Your family are the gatekeepers. This—" she held up the compass, "It's useless. At least with him," she said, pointing at Gramps.

"But *you*—"

Gramps moved quicker than I'd ever seen, like—like he was me. He'd never before shown he had the same abilities I had, other than seeing in the dark and sometimes sensing things. I'd never seen his speed.

He snatched the compass from the woman and tossed it to me just as he was hit again.

I caught it and looked up at the three men he tussled with, my friends' terrified eyes, Finch's grin growing larger, and the woman's look of a mix of astonishment and excitement.

"Do it," Gramps yelled as he fought. Some of the men were heading for me.

I backed up. What did he expect me to do? Was I supposed to run? I didn't know what he wanted. So I did the only thing I knew to do.

"Storey," I shouted with all my might.

For a split second, I had a heightened sense of everything. The air whipping around my body, sounds, and the damp smell of the trees and plants. My hand tightened around the compass.

An explosion of light blinded everyone.

"Go!" Gramps yelled, no longer sounding like his strong-self due to his injuries.

Go? This time the compass didn't lift me. I listened to him and ran toward the wavering light as it expanded. I couldn't see anything around me, but I kept going, running blind.

Suddenly, I could see. I was no longer in the woods. Buildings shimmered like water glistening in the sun. I stood on a walkway above the trees that reminded me of the shiny marbles I kept in a sack at home. Colorful blossoms filled the vined rails. I looked below at a turquoise river. *I'm here! Oh my gosh!* Gramps's descriptions of Storey had not done it justice.

"Welcome, Luella. You have made it home." said a woman, approaching me with her arms outstretched.

She knows my name?

I don't know what got into me. I was overcome with emotion and ran to her in tears. The woman, with skin like mine, was so tall. She wore a gold headdress with two thin cornrows in front that hung along the sides of her face down to her waist, and jewels surrounded her neck and arms.

With the grace of a ballerina, she knelt and embraced me. Her face looked as if light tried to escape from beneath her skin.

"You've done well," she said. "You could have turned back, but you didn't. You could've told everything you knew about Storey, but you kept it a secret."

About a hundred men wearing gold armor followed her—warriors.

"Who are you?"

She smiled down at me. "Your language would call me a Queen."

...

Seconds later, I stepped a gold-sandaled foot onto the forest floor.

"It's her! She's back!" said the woman.

But I wasn't alone. The warrior guards from Storey followed me.

"No!" the woman exclaimed while backing up. "Fire at will."

About half of those with her fired their weapons, but their bullets dropped to the ground. The others were frozen with fear as the gold-clad men walked up to them and picked up

Gramps. And like Gramps said, they were eight feet tall with bronze skin like his. A hand on his side glowed and healed him.

"No!" The woman yelled. "Take me!" She followed behind as they turned and walked away. The ground seemed to shake with each step. One of the men raised his hand as if he wanted her to high-five it. Then she walked forward and slammed into an invisible wall.

"At least leave a way for us to communicate," she pleaded.

In the second I was gone, I'd told them everything. Time passed differently in Storey. I'd bathed and been dressed in their style of clothing—a white tunic with gold beaded trim. Sparkling gold threads weaved through my hair, and even my skin glistened.

They shared the most amazing story with me. They said they'd been here all along, and we didn't even know it—guiding and testing me. Making sure I was worthy to join them along with Gramps. Seeing we would protect Storey at all costs.

One of the men spoke—not in English, but in the language I heard Gramps sing in sometimes. Only now did I understand it.

The woman picked herself up from the ground. "We still have your friends," she said.

The warrior from Storey who had spoken turned to them. "You may come home."

Robin was one of them. Finch was one of them. Wren was one of them. Even Ma Poo was one of them. All that time and we didn't even know it. She was there, helping raise me, knowing exactly where we came from because she was really from there too. They immediately disappeared in a cloud of gold ash.

The men that were with the white-haired woman fell to their knees. They'd only heard of the beings. Anyone old enough to remember when humans and the people of Storey were allies was already gone. It made me wonder how old Gramps really was. How old was I? What if we aged differently?

I guess I'd find out. We were home now.

We found the way to Storey. Or should I say, Storey found us.

The End

Let's Talk Storey

Discussion Questions

Discussion Questions

1. **Chapter 1**
   When Lou asked Gramps to tell her about Storey, he responded, "How do you get to Storey?" Do you think he knew something was going to happen to him?

2. **Chapter 2**
   When Gramps asked Lou, "Are you supposed to change because of what someone else thinks? Does a tiger change his stripes?" What did he mean?

3. **Chapter 3**
   Gramps didn't own a television or computer. Could you imagine your life without them? What would you do instead?

4. **Chapter 4**
   Did you ever not believe something someone told you? Did you do research to try and find out if what you were told was

true?

5. **Chapter 4**
   Why do you think Lou had never gone to a dentist?

6. **Chapter 5**
   When Gramps reminded Lou about following the birds, do you think he knew they were people (Robin, Finch, and Wren)?

7. **How do the people of Osowaw City** react toward Lou? What is Lou's reaction to the way they treat her? Do you feel it's acceptable to be treated that way?

8. **Chapter 8**
   When Lou told the class about swamp life, were you aware of the things she shared?

9. **An ecological role** is the importance or function that something plays in our ecosystem. Gramps taught Lou about the coyote's function in our ecosystem. Can you give an example of a type of ecosystem

and the plants and animals that may live there?

10. **Chapter 10**

    When Lou told the story of her making the fish jump into their boat, what did Gramps mean when he told her, "You need to understand the value in accomplishing something—working for what you have even though you don't have to"?

11. **Based on the entire book**, why do you think the people of Storey wanted nothing more to do with the people of Earth?

Please Leave A Review

Your review means the world to me. I greatly appreciate any kind words. Even one or two sentences go a long way. The number of reviews a book receives greatly improves how well it does on Amazon. Even a short review would be wonderful. Thank you in advance.

Turn the page for a preview of another book by L. B. Anne.

L. B. Anne

Gemma Kaine Sneak Peek

CHAPTER 1

"EEEYAAAAA! AAAIIIEEE!"

"Why exactly are you screaming and jumping on my couch?"

"I'm acting crazy. That's why I'm here, right? That's what everyone wants?"

He scratched the stubble on his jaw, propped his elbow on the arm of the chair, and rested his hand under his chin, before answering. He acted like he saw this stuff every day. But there was a twinkle in the big eye under his bushy brow—the right eye. The left was smaller and always squinting at her. "Who wants that, Gemma?"

"Who do you think?" Her sneakers hit the floor and she plopped down on the burgundy leather sofa, out of breath.

"You tell *me*."

"All of you," she replied while pulling a hair tie from her wrist and gathering her thick wavy hair into a low ponytail.

"No one has said that."

"I'm twelve years old. Kids don't wake up and say, 'Oh, I think I'll schedule an appointment to see a psychologist today.' So why am I here?"

"Well, I was hoping you'd tell me more about your dreams today."

Dr. Stanton sat so calmly, Gemma wished she could shoot him with a bolt of lightning or set firecrackers off under his chair to get a reaction or emotion out of him. Maybe if she snatched out one of the thin white hairs that hung from his nose, he would at least grimace or something.

It may not have seemed like it, but she didn't dislike him. There were good aspects to the sessions. During the last visit, he allowed her to yell out the worst word she could think of at the top of her lungs, so she'd feel comfortable.

Gemma sucked in a deep breath.

"VEGAN!" she'd screamed, released her balled fists, let her arms drop to her sides, and leaned back against the sofa. "That felt good," she'd said. That scream had been building up in her for a long time.

That was the first time she'd seen Dr. Stanton grin.

"—Your real dreams," he continued with a brow raised, as if she hadn't been truthful before.

"Those *are* my real dreams. I keep telling you Arsara really exists. It's a whole planet in another galaxy."

"Arsara? You've never given it a name before."

Gemma leaned toward him. "Air-sara. You have to roll the R's like in Spanish."

"Arsara," he repeated.

"Yes, that's it. Did you take Spanish? I got an A in that class because my pronunciation is on point. But Mr. Aviles didn't—"

"Please stay on the subject, Gemma."

"Sorry."

"Is there anything else you would like to tell me about Arsara?"

"I look different there."

"Different how?"

"I have purple hair, and grey eyes. Oh, and my skin is this brownish color. Not like the kind of peanutty color it is now," she said with a laugh. She'd never compared her brown skin to food before. "It's a weird tan color there. And there's this tattoo down my neck that's like henna. You know, like you might see on someone's hands."

"That's interesting," Dr. Stanton said with a nod.

"It's pretty cool. I have a family there, too."

"There?"

"On Arsara."

"What's wrong with your family here?"

Gemma threw her hands up in exasperation. "Nothing. That's not what I was—you're totally missing the point." She looked up at the shelves of books behind Dr. Stanton. It drove her crazy that they weren't organized by color. *I bet those are all for show. He's probably only read, like, five of them.*

An old bronze cocker spaniel bookend watched her as she ran a finger over the stack of books on the table beside her. Somehow it seemed out of place in such a modern office.

"Gemma, for our next session, I would like you to make a list of all the things you love about your family."

"The one on Arsara?"

"Your real family."

Gemma waited.

"What's wrong?"

"What else? It seemed like you were going to say something more."

"No. That's it."

"Well, what about all the things I dislike, because there's a lot—"

"Okay, make a list of those too, if you like."

"I'm going to need a poster board for that. I can email it."

"That isn't necessary. Bring the list with you next week."

"All right." She picked up her backpack and rose to leave.

"Gemma…" He always said her name and then paused a moment, as if he were thinking about what he was going to say next.

"Dr. Stanton…" Gemma replied, mimicking him.

"Before you fall asleep tonight, tell yourself there is no planet Arsara and that you're staying right where you are."

"You're not paying attention. I told you last time, I have no control over waking on Arsara. It's like sleep opens some kind of portal or something."

"I understand that. But give it a try."

There was no use arguing. No one believed her.

Gemma sighed and spoke softly. "Will do, Dr. Stanton." She placed her hands in her pockets and walked toward the door with her head low, studying the brown threads in the carpet.

Dr. Stanton opened the door, showing her out. Her mother had been reading a magazine in the waiting area and stood upon seeing her.

"We'll see you next week. Remember what I said," said Dr. Stanton.

Of course she would. That didn't mean she was going to do it. Gemma nodded, all the while flipping over the Perian in her pocket. Something actually came back with her this time.

CHAPTER 2

"Gemma, I'm parked right over there."

Her mother pointed across the street at the little blue car. "If you hadn't ridden your bike, I could give you a ride home." Their electric car was too tiny for her bike to fit.

Gemma always rode her bike to school and had gone straight from school to her appointment. "It's okay, I'd rather ride anyway."

Riding released the tension pushing at her brain from her sessions and gave her time to think. Plus, she liked feeling the breeze on her face as she rode as fast as possible, maneuvering around pedestrians. She could be a bit of a daredevil at times and looked for anything she could use as a takeoff ramp to practice her bunny hops. Although, it would be much easier to do with the BMX bike she begged her parents for, instead of her ten-speed.

"I'll meet you at home?" Her mom kissed her on the forehead, rubbed her hair, and rested her hand there for a moment.

She looked up at her mother's perfectly freckled face. The tiny specks mostly covered her nose and cheeks. Gemma used to joke that her mom had more than enough freckles to share with her daughter, so why didn't she get any. She also didn't get her mother's straight hair, or her dad's dark bronze complexion. She was somewhere in the middle of the two, but in her opinion, she didn't look much like either one.

"Mom, don't zone out on me. It's so weird," she said as she inserted her cell phone in her bike phone mount.

"I'm not zoning out. Get going, you."

"I'll beat you there," she replied with a grin.

Gemma placed her headphones on—the bone conduction kind. Her father insisted on those because she could listen to music and still hear what was happening around her. She adjusted her backpack on her back and unlocked her turquoise bike as No Doubt's "Just a Girl" pounded in her head. The lyrics resonated with her. *I've had it up to here too.*

Her foot kicked the kickstand back and she pedaled down the sidewalk, avoiding the subway grates and sidewalk cellar doors. She had a fear of falling through those after hearing about that happening to a kid on the news.

At certain times of day, New York sidewalks were almost as busy as the streets. Gemma would've preferred to ride on the street, but because she was only twelve, she had to stay on the sidewalk. Although, if she didn't tell anyone she was twelve, would they know? She could be a tiny adult. Maybe the giveaway was the cat ears sticking out of her psychedelic-peace-signed-kitty-faced bicycle helmet.

"On your left," she yelled as she stood on her pedals, approached a couple, and then swerved to the right, avoiding a group of people wearing business suits coming toward her. She held her breath, not wanting to inhale the cigarette smoke from one of them as she sailed by.

"Mr. Kolwaski! Up top!" she yelled to the bakery

owner, as she raised her hand in the air and he slapped it.

At the next corner, she came to an abrupt stop and looked around. A short line of people stood at the curb.

Should I, or shouldn't I?

"Are you in line?" a guy wearing an orange safety vest asked.

Am I? No, I'm not. I can't. "Yes," she replied proudly.

"Next!" yelled the man behind the cart in the street.

"One hot dog," Gemma yelled from the sidewalk.

The stand was covered in pictures of hot dogs and hot pretzels. Condiments, sodas, and juices littered the top, protected from the sun by an oversized yellow umbrella. Bags of potato chips hung along the side.

"What do you want on it?"

She turned to the construction worker-looking guy behind her. "What do you get on yours?"

He removed an earbud headphone from his ear with fingers that looked too pudgy to grasp it. "What did you say?"

"I asked what you get on yours?"

"Oh, everything."

Everything? Like I should get something more than mustard and ketchup?

"Everything," she said with confidence.

"Everything? You're saying you want onions; you want sauerkraut, you want pickled—"

"No. Scratch that. Mustard and ketchup."

"I'm just sayin. I *thought* that was too much," he replied in a thick New York accent, without looking up. He took Gemma's crumpled dollars and handed her a hot dog.

"Keep the change," she said as she and walked along with her bike, inhaling the scent of the smoky meat. She stopped near a fruit stand and lifted it to her mouth.

To the right of her, a car's brakes screeched. "Gemma!" her mother shouted.

Gemma watched her and brought the hotdog closer to her lips.

The car door swung open. "Gemma, don't you dare. Drop the hotdog, young lady!"

Panic covered Gemma's face. Her mother was about to walk through traffic to stop her. She considered making a run for it but didn't think she could ride her bike fast enough with one hand holding the hotdog. She could drop her bike, dash to an alley, duck behind some trash bins, and have her first bite ever of processed meat—any kind of meat. Instead, Gemma froze and then opened her hand, releasing the hot dog. It dropped to the ground, splattering mustard on her shoe while she stared at her mother with her mouth open.

She grabbed her handlebars and began to pedal away.

"Pick that up," her mother yelled, as car horns blared behind her.

Gemma backed up, picked up the hotdog, and placed it in a trash bin. *How does she always catch me? I mean, if I'm allergic to meat, just tell me. My dad is going to flip. I was already caught. I should have at least taken a bite.*

"Get home, right now!"

Sheesh. Do you have to embarrass me in front of everyone in earshot? She looked back. A teen boy held his cell phone up at her, filming it all, and smiled with satisfaction.

"You weren't hungry, were you?" asked a girl that

walked past wearing a satin bomber jacket and torn jeans. She glanced up from her phone just for a second to make sure Gemma heard her.

Gemma clawed her fingers, threw her head back, and groaned. She hardly ever saw kids from school, but here was Griselle of all people. At the worst possible moment.

There was no time to stew in it. She had to beat her mother home. She rode fast. Her mom would still have to find a parking space, either in the garage or on the street. That gave her a few extra minutes.

"Hey, Gemma," said the lobby attendant as she hurried inside. "I can take your bike for you if you like."

"Thanks, Hector. I appreciate it. I've got to get upstairs."

He rolled it behind the counter. "I figured as much."

The doors of the elevator slid open just as she approached it.

"Gemma!"

"Mrs. Feldman, I was just coming to get the boys. Sorry, I'm late."

"If you don't want the job, Gemma—"

Three black pugs ran out of the elevator in a hurry to get outside. Mrs. Feldman held the leash out toward Gemma.

"I do want the job. Oh, you've been to the salon today?"

Mrs. Feldman really enjoyed when you noticed things about her. Gemma hoped that would get her back on her good side. "That's a pretty color," she said of her manicured nails as the pugs padded over the terrazzo floor, pulling toward the exit.

"Oh, thank you, Gemma. The nail tech told me fuchsia makes me look like a youngster," she said with a laugh. "Ira never notices."

The pugs yanked her away. "We'll be back," Gemma yelled behind her.

"She's always late, that one," Mrs. Feldman told Hector.

Mrs. Feldman was a chronic complainer. The quicker Gemma got out of there, the less she'd have to hear. Today, Gemma would be the subject of her complaints to anyone she could get to stop and listen. The day before, her quibble was about the deli, her doctor, something about not being superstitious, and a boil on Ira's—Mr. Feldman's—neck. Gemma ignored it all. She tended to block out over-talkers. It was her superpower.

As the happy pugs ran over each other and pulled Gemma through the lobby, her mother entered, looking irritated. Her expression changed, seeing the dogs.

"I'll see you shortly," she said and held her hand out to take Gemma's backpack from her.

Gemma knew what those four words meant. What she was really saying was, "We're going to sit down for a little talk when you get home." Her parents would do all the talking, and she'd sit sulking.

There was no way out of it, so Gemma did the only thing she could do. She made the walk last as long as possible while she thought out a good argument. As a result, the pugs got plenty of exercise and Mrs. Feldman got her money's worth.

"Goodbye, Lola, Lily, Max," Gemma said to the pugs as she knelt in front of Mrs. Feldman's door. "You'll probably never see me again, because my dad is going to kill me." Max began to whine. She hugged him. "I'll be okay, Max. I was just joking. I'm sure I'll think of something. But come and find me if they lock me away in a dungeon."

The pugs ran inside, and Gemma grudgingly entered the elevator to go up to her floor. She stood there staring at the wall and the elevator started moving because she'd taken too long to push the button for her floor. It lowered to the lobby.

"Gemma!" the girl exclaimed as the doors opened.

"Hey, Sash!"

Sasha was one of Gemma's few friends that lived in her building. Italian, feisty, and a year older than Gemma. She wiped her mouth on the back of her hand and rubbed it on the side of her over-sized Just Let Me Live t-shirt.

The remnants of something were still on her face, either frosting, mayo, or whipped cream.

"Are your parents still planning to send you to that camp this summer?"

"Let's call it what it is, Gem Marie." Sasha made up middle names for everyone she knew. "A fat farm. But I'm on this new diet, and I'm doing pretty good."

"Oh really?" Gemma almost laughed. Sasha never stuck to her diets.

"Yeah, I'm vegan now, but I eat meat too."

"That's not vegan."

"Yes, it is—a different kind. Just like there are different kinds of vegetarians."

"Not vegan."

She rolled her eyes. "And no sweets."

Gemma touched the side of her mouth and Sasha followed suit, feeling the crumbs on her face.

"Oh."

"Whatcha got?"

Sasha held a plastic bag filled with water and tied at the top. She held the bag up at face level.

"What's in there?" Gemma looked closer. "Oh wow, those are tiny shrimp. What happened to your goldfish, Creole?"

"We are not going to discuss that."

Gemma ran her finger across the bag.

"Hey, do that again. Are they following your finger?"

Gemma ran her finger in the opposite direction and the shrimp followed. "That's so weird."

She was still staring at the tiny beige shrimp when

the elevator stopped on her floor.

The doors opened and Sasha put her arm out to keep them from closing. "So?"

"So what?"

"You know what. How was your visit with the shrink? Did you get shrunk?"

"I don't think they like being called that."

"Well, are you still crazy?" She laughed.

Gemma crossed her eyes and made a face at her. "I was never crazy."

"Yeah, I know."

"If I'm crazy, I'm crazy for being your friend," Gemma said and stepped off the elevator.

"No. That's called luck!"

The elevator door closed.

"Call me later," Sasha yelled at the last second.

Gemma stood outside her apartment a moment, staring at the black door, before unlocking it. It squealed as it opened, and light from the hallway poured into their dim foyer.

"Gemma, come and sit down," a rich deep voice said as she hung her bike helmet on its hook. Her father was already home. She didn't expect that. *How am I going to get out of this one*, she thought as she bit her lip. She could start a conversation about his album collection and Bob Marley. That might soften him up a bit. Might.

Gemma removed her shoes and put them on the bottom shelf of the hall cabinet. Their home was always neat and in order. White walls, sparse white furniture, and lots of plants. Gemma often joked their decor style was modern jungle.

They owned tons of books. Her father was a professor and a scholar of aerospace. It wasn't uncommon for him to receive a call from NASA. Which was why Dr. Stanton felt she came up with the planet Arsara. Because she was around space stuff all the time.

Though she tried to take her time, the next room was only a few steps down the hall. She turned into the living room, where her father sat in his favorite chair, as straight as a board. He never relaxed. He faced the window, his ebony skin glistening in the sunlight, and ran his hand over his beard.

Her mother had been in the kitchen but walked in and stood at his side.

"Hi, Dad."

Gemma kissed him on the cheek and sat across from him on the sofa. He waited while Gemma studied the cuffs of her jeans and then looked up at him. After all the things she'd rehearsed to say, she couldn't remember any of it. "I just wanted to taste one. Why do you act like that's a crime?"

"Gemma, we do not eat flesh!"

"Why can't I? It's my fifth amendment. My freedom of eat!"

"This is not the time for your witticism. I assume you are referencing the first amendment and freedom of speech."

"And why do you talk like that? 'Gemma, we do not eat flesh,'" she repeated, mimicking him. "It's just meat. People eat meat, you know? And no one talks like that. You speak like you're a— Like you're a— a—" She tried to think of what her father reminded her of.

"Like I'm a what?" he asked, curious.

"Royalty or something." Her father reminded her of a king—a leader of some secret African tribe. He sat so straight, like he'd been raised to be a king and sit on a throne. And they acted like she'd done something beneath the royal family.

Her parents glanced at each other. "These are simple rules, Gemma."

"I know. I'm sorry. I threw the hot dog away."

"Have our meals not been satisfying to you?"

He's still talking like that. "I don't know. They've been fine, I guess."

Her father's eyes narrowed. He preferred she was direct when she spoke.

She huffed. "I mean, Mom's meals are really good. I just— I just wondered." Gemma's voice trailed off. She knew how serious her parents were about her not eating meat and wondered what they'd told her school that would make the lunch lady not give it to her and someone stop her if she were to attempt a bite of her friend's hamburger. Someone was always watching.

"May I go to my room now?"

"Dinner is ready."

"I'm not hungry. May I be excused?"

Her mother looked at her father and he nodded.

Gemma stood, shaking her head. They had just covered items number one and two on her list of what she didn't like about her family. She couldn't eat what she wanted, and the way her mom waited for her dad's okay. *What century is this? Sheesh!*

Gemma sat on her bed and reached in her pocket. The greenish-blue Perian stone sparkled like it had specks of glitter inside. To anyone else, the Perian was sure to look like just a glass rock—something man-made. She held it up to the light. What if she could bring back more? But what would bringing things back prove to anyone other than her? First, she needed to figure out how she was able to go to Arsara in the first place. Then she could prove to her parents she wasn't crazy, and they could stop with all the whispering and looking at her in that suspicious way.

She set the Perian beside her. She liked Arsara and didn't mind going there. But what if she got stuck and couldn't get back home?

CHAPTER 3

Gemma climbed into her bed and looked up at the white canopy with flowing sheer curtains that draped down on either side of the head of her bed. The Perian was proof she wasn't crazy. Still, she spoke Dr. Stanton's words. "There is no planet Arsara, and I'm staying where I am. Right here in my bed," she said while patting her mattress with her palm.

She turned on her side facing her window, looking up at the stars, as a slight breeze blew through the open window. Thin white curtains glided back, allowing the gentle wind to find her.

Her eyes closed as she listened to the faint sound of a trumpet; jazz music floated in from another apartment, lulling her.

Moments later, Gemma scratched her head and swatted at something buzzing around her ear. Her hand hit a wall. She reached up high, feeling the smooth alcove, and turned over with a smile on her face.

I'm here, she thought as she pushed her thick purple hair out of her face, and flipped her orange-tan hands over, examining them. Her nails were the same color.

"Seha, rise. The day's giving awaits."

"I will, Ahme!" Gemma replied, but didn't move. *Wait for it, wait for it.*

Suddenly, she jumped up and faced the outer room. "Ya!" she exclaimed as Galoot charged at her. He stopped just short of her, clumsily rolled over, and ran the other way, knowing she'd chase after him.

"Aye! Seha!" her Arsarian mother exclaimed as Gemma ran past her, spinning her around. Galoot ran between her legs and she almost tripped over him.

The large eared animal was Gemma's pet; a wartle. A gentle creature of Arsara, and probably

Gemma's best friend, since she did everything with him by her side. She squatted and scratched Galoot's leathery wrinkled skin behind his ears. He yelped with delight. Wartles appeared hairless, but if you looked closely, there were fine tiny hairs all over it.

A strong hand seized the back of Gemma's garment and pointed to the door…

To continue reading, get your copy of *Gemma Kaine Sky Rider.*

Other Books by L. B. Anne:

Curly Girl Adventures Series:
Pickled Pudding
Zuri the Great
Tangled
Top Knot (coming soon)

Lolo And Winkle Series:
Go Viral
Zombie Apocalypse Club
Frenemies
Break London
Middle School Misfit
The Compete Collection

Brave New World:
Gemma Kaine: Sky Rider
Gemma Kaine: The Curse of Mantlay (coming soon)

Everfall Series:
Before I Let Go
If I fail

The Sheena Meyer Series:
The Girl Who Looked Beyond the Stars
The Girl Who Spoke to the Wind
The Girl Who Captured the Sun
The Girl Who Became a Warrior
City of Gleamers (coming soon)

Snicker's Wish: A Christmas Story

ABOUT THE AUTHOR

L. B. Anne is best known for her Sheena Meyer book series about a girl with a special gift, and a destiny that can save the world. L. B. Anne lives on the Gulf Coast of Florida with her husband and is a full-time author, speaker, and mental health advocate. When she's not inventing new obstacles for her diverse characters to overcome, you can find her reading, playing bass guitar, running on the beach, or downing a mocha iced coffee at a local cafe while dreaming of being your favorite author. Visit L. B. at www.lbanne.com

Facebook: facebook.com/authorlbanne
Instagram: Instagram.com/authorlbanne
Twitter: twitter.com/authorlbanne
Pinterest: pinterest.com/AuthorLBAnne

Made in the USA
Las Vegas, NV
09 November 2022